THE CHOSEN

JILL SANDERS

GRAYTON PRESS

DIGITAL ISBN: 978-1-945100-33-8

PRINT ISBN: 978-8470728319

Copyeditor: Erica Ellis – inkdeepediting.com

SUMMARY

Tara's parents had always told her that she was special. But until her sixteenth birthday, she never knew just how special she was. Coming into powers had been the last thing on her to-do list. Especially after her parents' disappearance on that fateful night. Now, almost ten years later, she's learned how to hide her gifts and that it's best to keep to herself. Which means a life on the run, moving anytime she slips up. And she tends to slip up—a lot.

All Colt wants to do is complete his latest job so he can take some well-deserved time off. But this mark was proving to be a slippery one. After more than a decade in special ops, bringing one helpless woman in should be the easiest job ever. But after a bump-in with the blonde, something strange happens to him. He no longer cares about the job.

PROLOGUE

Tara smiled down at the soft-pink cake with its sixteen perfectly placed sparkling pink candles and smiled.

Her friends, the select few that she'd deemed worthy to attend such an elite event, cheered around her as the fairy lights that had been strung overhead twinkled around them all.

The entire yard had been transformed into a magical fairy-tale wonderland. Just for her. A long table of gifts sat on the porch, ready for her to open after everyone had some cake and punch.

There was a DJ playing all of their favorite songs and a dance floor and flashing lights. No one had dared step out on it, since the party wasn't in full swing just yet.

As she blew out the candles, she silently made a wish that Hunter McCann would ask her to dance tonight.

But the moment the last candle's light disappeared, the sky above her lush hillside home suddenly darkened. Then the wind kicked up, sending decorations flying as everyone scurried to seek shelter from the lightning and rain.

Tara stood in the center of the yard and cursed the freak weather as everyone ran for shelter. The rain was ruining her perfect party. The water soaked the designer silk dress that she'd convinced her stepmother to splurge on just for the special occasion.

Why was this happening to her? Couldn't it rain on some less-popular person's birthday instead? She stomped her foot in frustration and, suddenly, the ground shook. She screamed, and so did everyone else at her party as the sky grew even darker. Silently wishing for everything to go back to the way it was, she pouted and closed her eyes momentarily as the shaking grew harder.

Then she watched in horror as the wind and rain gathered around her, as if surrounding only her. It pelted her face, soaked her completely, and lifted her long blonde hair, tangling it around her face.

She pushed her hair aside just in time to see the hillside where her beautiful home sat vanish into thin air before her eyes.

Crying out, she reached for everyone, for her parents, her friends. But as if in a terrible end-of-the-world movie, she watched in horror as fear crossed all their faces while they faded into nothingness.

When the wind finally died down less than a minute later, she stood in her ruined party dress, with her hair soaking wet, on a patch of perfectly green grass. A large blinding light hovered above her in the night sky.

Evening had somehow turned into night just as quickly as everything she'd loved had faded before her eyes.

She had to blink a few times to assure herself that she was all alone and that the light high above her was real. And that everything she cared about was truly gone.

When she looked around, she couldn't see any signs that

her home had ever existed in this place. The hillside she stood on appeared to be the same one where she'd grown up, where the stone building she'd always called home had just stood.

Half expecting a pile of wood, stone, and cement to be in the place where her home had sat, she turned and saw... nothing. Just grass, trees, and wildflowers.

The scariest part was the massive singular moon hovering high above her. The light from it almost blinded her, and she could barely see the twinkle from the stars that she knew so well. Were they all gone too?

She sank down into the soft grass and cried until her head ached. She must have fallen asleep at one point and when she woke it was dawn. She stood up, dusted off her dress, and began to search the area for any sign of her family, her friends. What felt like hours later, when her voice had grown hoarse from calling out to them, she sat down in the grass and cried again, this time for everything she'd just lost. Not because of the horror of the day—for the loss of her parents, her friends, her life—but because she was now all alone.

Tara woke with a start, shaken from the nightmare. The memory. Her first thought was to run. To hide. She felt tears streaming down her face. Then she heard the hum of the cars passing her by on the highway and remembered where she was—in her travel van on the side of the road.

She looked out the window and the sight of the many stars lighting up the darkness of the desert night calmed her until she relaxed back.

Closing her eyes, she wished the memory would disappear just as everyone that day had.

It had taken her close to a week to find someone to help her. She'd walked through the woods until she'd stumbled upon a cabin. When she'd told the police what had happened, they'd glanced at one another and snickered. Then they'd accused her of fabricating the entire story.

They'd asked her for her name and address, and she'd been shocked when they informed her that there was no such place. That her home had never existed.

When they told her that there had never been a Jason and Robin Dawson living in the state, she'd mentally broken down. They had quickly marked her as a runaway and sent her to a halfway home for troubled teens.

For years she tried to get anyone to believe her, but there were no bodies and no sign of her childhood home, so no one did.

Tara had, in the span of less than a dozen heartbeats, gone from the princess on the hill, living in a castle with anything she could ever dream of at her fingertips, to a pauper living in a hovel with a dozen or more degenerates.

Her childhood had been filled with expensive gifts, toys, and everything she'd ever wanted. She'd been so spoiled that she'd never had to do a chore in her life. Now, she not only had chores she was expected to do each day, but shortly after arriving, she'd been told to get a paying job. She had to purchase her own clothing and her own food, all while fending off the aggressive kids she lived with, who tried to steal what she'd worked hard for.

Now Tara rolled over and tried to block the images of her past out of her mind. Only they wouldn't leave. She knew what could happen if she continued down this train of thought.

She tossed off the blankets, climbed to the front of the sleeper van, and started up the engine. If she couldn't sleep, she might as well drive.

Here it was, ten years later, and she was still all alone. Less than a year after moving into the halfway home, she'd packed a bag and set out on her own. Anything had to be better than living like that.

They'd called her a runaway from that first day, so why not make it true? After all, she'd been seventeen at the time and making enough money to support herself.

It hadn't been difficult, moving to the street. Not after she'd lost everything that fateful first day.

She'd actually welcomed the change. Welcomed being dependent on herself and not others. She was even good at it, fending for herself.

The first thing she'd done was leave California. She hated the weather, the people, the expensive things. It reminded her too much of everything she'd lost.

At first, it had made her skin crawl to be treated as less than human by people who had what she used to have. Had she treated people like that when she'd been in their position? Probably. That made her stomach hurt even more.

After leaving California, she'd hitchhiked up to Seattle and had gotten a job as a barista. She found a roommate and for at least the first year had lived a pretty normal life.

Then, one evening, she'd missed the bus to her apartment and had stomped her foot in frustration. When a large split in the pavement appeared in front of her, she had blinked a few times in disbelief. Then the ground had started to shake and, this time, she'd run for her life, unwilling to lose everything once more.

She'd packed her things in a backpack and hadn't stopped moving until she'd ended up in Utah almost a month later. Again, she'd found a job in a coffee shop in a small town, this time as a manager.

She'd gotten the job when she'd walked in to get a cup of coffee and the only employee had been overwhelmed, so she'd stepped in the back to help out. The owner had shown up less than an hour later and hired her on the spot.

The nice older woman had rented her the room above the coffee shop, and she'd stuck around the small town for almost a full year.

She'd been sitting outside on one of her many breaks one day and happened to see a young couple kissing on the corner. Watching the couple, her heart had yearned for a boyfriend, for anyone to be close to. The next thing she'd known, the old brick building was shaking. Glass windowpanes broke, cars veered off the road and hit parked cars, people screamed, and Tara knew exactly what was happening. She knew it was time to move on.

That was the day she stopped wishing for anything. Stopped hoping that someday she'd have someone in her life, that she could possibly be normal. That was the day she realized there was something wrong with her.

From that day forward, strange things continued to happen, ensuring that she never stayed in one place for too long.

She'd ended up in Denver one snowy night and had gotten a flat tire. Pulling off to the side of the road, she realized she'd never changed a tire in her life.

Doing her best, she jacked up the van that she'd purchased a year earlier and had just removed the flat tire to put on the spare when the jack slipped. The entire van came rushing towards her, but then she'd stopped it. Just like that, she was holding the weight of the entire van in her hands as if it weighed no more than a feather.

After putting the jack back in place, she'd finished changing the tire quickly. The next morning, she'd convinced herself that she'd dreamed the whole thing.

That week she'd broken into an empty hunting cabin and had tried a few things out. She pushed herself beyond what she thought was possible. Each time she did something unfeasible, she wrote it down in a notebook.

For ten years, every time she forgot herself for a moment or let her guard down and someone noticed it, she was forced to jump in her secondhand sleeper van, which held all her worldly possessions, and flee.

She'd tried once to get close to people. To let her guard down. That fiasco had almost cost her everything, so she stopped trying to make friends. To find someone to get close to. She settled, at least in her mind, upon being alone for the rest of her life.

Recently, she'd read a few old articles and had gotten the idea to head south. To Hidden Creek, Georgia, to be exact.

The place sounded eerie. She was especially intrigued by a story about a woman named Xtina Warren, who, according to the article, had extraordinary abilities. Nothing like hers, but it was a start.

While she made her way south from Washington, she researched everything she could about the woman and the town. By the time she made it to Georgia, she'd read all about Xtina and her close circle of friends, thanks to a few articles written by Breanna Garrett-Kincaid.

Some of the articles were hard to believe, but others not so much after what she'd been through in the past years. Her one hope was that she'd find answers to what was happening to her. If Xtina and her friends didn't have any insights into what was going on, then she was truly alone in this world.

CHAPTER 1

From the moment Tara drove into Hidden Creek, Georgia, she felt something shift in her core. There was power here. She wasn't sure what kind of energy it was, but it caused her entire body to go on guard and vibrate.

Parking in front of the one and only coffee shop, she debated her next step. She was running incredibly low on supplies and money. She had less than fifty dollars hidden in her boot.

She was low on gas and it had been days since she'd eaten a full meal. She'd been getting by on a handful of stale cracker packets from the last diner she'd worked at and junk food she purchased at gas stations along the way.

If she didn't find answers in town, she was going to have to do something drastic and find someplace more permanent to settle down. Most likely a city where there were an abundance of jobs and loads of people to blend in with.

She checked herself in the mirror, then pulled out some wipes and cleaned her face. She dabbed some deodorant on, sprayed herself with the cheap perfume she'd purchased at a mall, and then braided her long blonde hair. She wouldn't win any beauty contests, but at least she looked pretty enough to get a job at a small-town coffee shop.

The moment she stepped out of her van, she felt a wave of power rush through her. Why the hell couldn't she just be normal?

She was pretty sure that her hair and fingertips were sparking with the burst of energy she felt pulsing through her. She took several deep breaths, straightened her spine, and walked through the doors of the Coffee Corner.

She hadn't expected the woman behind the counter to stop what she was doing and smile at her.

"Good, you're finally here. Come on, then." The blonde-haired woman motioned behind her. "We're backed up."

"I…" Tara glanced around. Sure enough, there were more than half a dozen people in line waiting to place their orders. Everyone turned to look at her, and her heart rate spiked. Some had annoyed looks on their faces, as if upset that she wasn't hurrying behind the counter to make their morning drinks. Others looked at her like most did a stranger in their small hometown.

Since more than several of those people were looking at her with annoyance and impatience, she moved closer to the woman behind the counter.

"I'm not…" she started to say, but the woman just shook her head.

"There's an apron just inside that door." The woman waved towards the double swinging doors. "We need three lattes, one mochaccino, a skinny latte, and an espresso. Think you can handle that?"

Without missing a beat, Tara nodded.

"Good." The woman waved her hands and turned back to take the customer's money.

Grabbing the apron, Tara took a quick moment to look in the back of the coffee shop and noted another employee rushing around doing dishes.

When Tara was done with the first order, she took the tickets for the next order and got to work while the bell over the door kept indicating new customers flooding in.

How could such a small town have so many people wanting coffee at this time of day? How had the woman dealt with all of this herself before she'd come in?

It was half an hour before there was finally a long enough break in the orders that she could talk to the woman.

"So, what's your name?" the woman asked, leaning against the counter as she sipped an iced tea.

"Tara," she answered. "I think there's been—"

"No mistake." The woman smiled. "I'm Jess St. Clair."

"Tara Dawson," she answered.

Jess gave her a big smile. "Welcome to Hidden Creek by the way."

"Thanks," Tara said, unsure of how to move forward after this. Should she tell the woman she was making a mistake or just go along with it, in hopes that she could maybe at least get a free meal and a cup of coffee for her time.

"Want a cup of something and a muffin?" Jess motioned to the display case. "Help yourself."

It was almost eerie how the woman seemed to know what she was thinking ahead of time.

"Thanks, it's just…" Tara tried to start again.

"You do want the job, right?" Jess asked with a smile.

"Yes." It almost burst from her.

Jess chuckled. "Good, then it's settled." She grabbed a chocolate muffin and an orange juice from the cold case and set them in front of Tara.

Tara twisted the cap off and took a swig of the juice and realized it was just what she'd needed. She'd craved the coffee, but the juice soothed the thirst and the need for sugar. She took a nibble of the muffin and held in a groan of appreciation.

"So, welcome aboard." Jess held out her hand. Reaching out, Tara took her hand easily. Whatever sort of mistake this was, she was going to enjoy it while she could.

The moment their skin touched, Tara felt an electric pulse zip through her. Her vision grayed until she saw an image of three women chanting words Tara didn't understand. Then the flash was gone just as quickly as it had come.

"Interesting," Jess said, tilting her head slightly as her eyes narrowed.

The bell above the door chimed, and she watched Jess transform. Her smile brightened as she rushed around the counter to greet a police officer holding a small boy about a year old in his arms.

Seeing the man in uniform, Tara tensed and shrank back.

"There are my men," Jess said cheerfully as she took the child from the cop.

If she hadn't been so concerned about this exposure to the law, she would have spent more time appreciating the man in uniform. He was tall and dark haired, and had a sexy-as-sin grin on his face as he looked at Jess. As it was, she turned and tried to busy herself by wiping down the countertop.

"Is this her?" the cop asked, getting her attention.

"It is. This is Tara. Tara, my husband, Jacob, and our son, Reed." Jess shifted the child on her hip and walked behind the counter to hand the kid a small biscuit, which the boy immediately shoved in his mouth.

Tara warded off the desire to run away and instead walked over and nodded towards Jacob. The man ran his eyes over her, and her heart skipped several times.

It wasn't as if she was wanted by the police. Not that she knew of, at any rate. She had run away from the halfway house when she'd been seventeen, but that had been ten years ago, and she was well within her legal rights to be out on her own. Besides, she doubted anyone at the shelter had called the cops when she'd disappeared.

Okay, so she was driving without a license and the van's registration was a few years out of date. Hell. How was she supposed to get it registered when she didn't have a physical address in the first place? She had tried to register it in a few different states that claimed they didn't need permanent addresses, but they had required her to have a license, and for that she had to have an address.

So, she was breaking the law… but only a little since she'd put down a PO Box address and the clerk hadn't picked up on it.

"Nice to meet you," she said clearly, holding in her worries.

"Likewise. Jess was pretty excited about you coming into town," Jacob said, surprising Tara.

"She was?" Tara glanced over at Jess, who was bouncing her son on her hip, watching Tara closely.

"Yeah, she kept telling me that she couldn't wait to finally have someone in town capable of making a good cup of Java besides her." He nodded. "I told her I'd believe it when I tasted it. Which brings me to my order…" He smiled at her, and she relaxed. Okay, so small-town cop wasn't going to hound her for her credentials.

"What's your poison?" she asked easily.

While she made Jacob's brew, she listened to the couple talk, trying hard to overhear what they were talking about. It wasn't until she'd set down his drink that she heard them mention Xtina.

"You know Xtina?" She hadn't meant to ask that out loud, but when the pair stopped and turned to her, she blushed. "I, um, read an article about her a while back."

Jess smiled at her. "Yes, Xtina's my best friend. She and the rest of the gang are eager to meet you."

"Me?" Tara asked with a frown.

Jess nodded and then sighed. "I don't want to scare you off, but..." Just then the bell above the door chimed again, and Jess glanced over.

The man who stepped into the building looked familiar somehow. His dark hair was cut short, military style. He was easily as tall as Jacob was, reaching about six-two or more. Where the cop had a lean build, this man had wide, thick muscles and very tan skin. Like he spent a lot of time outdoors.

When his eyes moved over her, she felt her skin prickle with sexual awareness. She may have been on the run for years, but that didn't mean she was dead. But one thing in her life was certain—all of her relationships, friendship or sexual, had been casual and short lived.

Here was a man she could sink her teeth into, at least for a while. She stood as if a statue, watching the man approach the counter and look up at the menu that hung overhead.

"Good," Jess said with a sigh as she handed her son back to Jacob. "Everyone's finally here." She leaned over and gave her son and husband a kiss. "We'll see you later."

Tara frowned at Jess's words. What did she mean everyone was finally here? How had she and Xtina known she was coming into town?

Could all the articles she'd read be true? Or was this all some sort of joke Jess was playing on her? Besides, there was still a possibility that Jess had mistaken her for someone else.

Jacob glanced quickly at the man who had just walked

into the place and was looking at the menu with a slight frown. "You sure about this?" Jacob asked Jess.

"Always," Jess said and then waved her husband off. "Go on. You don't want to be late dropping Reed off at Xtina and Mike's."

Jacob shifted his son, grabbed the coffee mug, and took a quick sip. "Good coffee," Jacob said, motioning with his cup. "Jess was right, once again." With this, he walked out of the building, holding his son.

"You'll want to start a café latte," Jess said quietly before turning around to greet the newcomer. "Morning," Jess said as Tara started making the drink. "Welcome to Hidden Creek. How about a scone and a latte?"

Glancing over her shoulder, she watched surprise flash in the man's sexy amber eyes.

"That… sounds perfect," he answered. Even his voice was sexy as hell.

She finished making the drink and walked over to set it down next to the scone Jess had plated. This time, when her eyes locked with the man's, she knew she'd seen him before, but wasn't sure when and where.

"Do I know you?" she asked suddenly.

The man seemed surprised and then embarrassed. "I… think we ran into each other in the gas station just outside of Atlanta," he replied.

She thought back and then realized he'd been standing in the line for the checkout, directly in front of her.

"Right." She nodded. "Coke and Funyuns."

He chuckled. "Travel food." He rolled his eyes. "I'm hoping this is much better." He motioned to the coffee and the scone. She nodded slightly and turned but stopped when he said, "That's a long trip to come to work."

She glanced over at Jess, who smiled.

"I… just started working here," she admitted.

"Oh, well," the man said, seeming slightly stumped, "so you live in town then?"

She felt her entire body heat. She hadn't been expecting questions like this yet. She'd hoped to just get a job, then determine a place to park her van at night.

"I… do for now." She turned away to clean the counter once more.

"How about you?" Jess asked the man. "Are you just passing through?"

Glancing over her shoulder, she saw the man turn his attention to Jess again.

"I haven't decided yet," he said as he paid.

"Well, if you need a place to stay, there's a great hotel that just opened up down the way," Jess said easily.

"Yeah, thanks," he said smoothly. "I'll have to check it out."

The man walked over and sat in the booth.

"Are you always this nice to strangers?" Tara asked.

Jess laughed. "To me, there are no strangers." Then she turned on her. "So we're having this thing tonight, and I think you should be there."

Tara's first inclination was to quickly make up some excuse why of she wouldn't go. After all, she was still having a difficult time believing all of this wasn't some sort of mistake. Then Jess reached over and touched her arm.

"Xtina really wants to meet you. But she's just given birth to her daughter, Harper, and is still pretty much housebound. Come, she…" She shook her head quickly. "We've all been expecting you."

"What does that even mean?" Tara asked.

Jess smiled. "Guess you'll have to find out tonight. Will you come?"

Tara had to admit, she'd worried about how she was going to meet Xtina before coming into town. She never would have believed she'd get so lucky so quickly after arriving in town. Besides, she was not only curious, she was downright desperate for answers. If this was her chance to get them, she wasn't going to pass it up.

"What time and where?" she asked.

hy had he allowed his stomach to lead him into the coffee shop? He should have crossed the street and sat in the diner, watching the place instead of following his mark into the coffee shop.

No, he'd had to follow the smell of fresh ground coffee and the pretty blonde inside half an hour after she'd come in to see what was taking her so long.

Seeing her behind the counter had been a slight shock. He had expected to see her sitting at a table, drinking a cup of coffee, not working. But that wasn't the only reason for his surprise. For once, she looked happy.

Her eyes were filled with joy instead of caution, as they'd been since he'd first tracked her down.

In the past month, he'd only gotten this close to her when he'd bumped into her at the gas station a few hours earlier. He'd turned around to pay for his items and she'd been there. But by the time he'd filled up his truck with gas, her van was nowhere in sight, and he'd hoped she'd continued in the same direction so he could catch up with her.

He'd been so close to her many times before, but each

time he'd found out that she'd just left town or had just quit one of her temporary jobs.

He honestly hadn't thought that she would remember him. It wasn't as if they'd talked to one another at the gas station.

After he'd finished his scone and his coffee, the woman who'd been talking to the cop when he'd walked in came over to his table.

"So, have you decided yet?" she asked him.

"Decided?"

"If you're going to stay in town or not."

"Oh." He glanced towards Tara, who was busy filling orders behind the counter. Her back was to him, that long blonde hair of hers in a single braid that lay over her shoulder.

He wondered if she was going to stick around the small town for more than a day. It wasn't often that she did, but when she found a job, she usually hung out longer. From the looks of it, she was going to stick around for at least one night, so he made a quick decision.

"I'm staying, at least for tonight," he replied.

The woman's smile brightened. "Good. I'm Jess by the way." She slid into the booth across from him smoothly. "You are?"

He glanced towards Tara and then back at Jess. "Colt," he answered.

"Colt, what brings you to Hidden Creek?" she asked, her eyes scanning his face.

"Work," he answered quickly.

"Oh, are you looking for a job too?"

"No, I have one. One that takes me all over." He hadn't really been prepared to answer any questions but figured he would follow the plan he had in place when things took a turn during a job.

"Oh? What do you do?" Jess asked, hanging onto his every word.

"Security," he said, knowing it was best to keep his answers vague.

"Oh." She tilted her head, and he understood she was waiting for more details.

"Private security. Was that your husband earlier?" He figured to turn the questions onto her. After all, asking questions and getting answers was the baseline of his work.

"Yes." Jess smiled and gave him a look that said she understood the game he was playing.

"And son?" he asked. She nodded. "Do you own the shop?" He glanced around and tried not to look over to where Tara was now watching them from behind the counter.

"Sort of," Jess answered. "What kind of security? My brothers-in-law have a private security company. They mainly work with online clients."

"Oh?" He was interested now.

"They co-own Kincaid Investigations. Mike started it, but Ethan joined the business less than a year later."

"Kincaid?" he asked, very interested now. "I've heard of them. They just earned the contract for Fanatics." Anyone and everyone in the private sector had heard the news. Fanatics was a large online temp job site that had popped up in the past few years.

"Yes," Jess said, and then she relaxed back against the booth, as if she'd been testing his knowledge. "Something tells me your type of security isn't just the cyber kind." Her eyes ran over him.

He knew what she and everyone else saw when he walked into a room. He was built like a linebacker. He had four years in special ops and hours and hours of downtime in the past few years that he'd spent lifting weights.

"I'm not really good with computers," he admitted.

"So…" She leaned onto the table and glanced around. "Who in Hidden Creek needs protection?"

He smiled. "Let's just say I'm very particular about keeping my clients' private affairs… private."

Jess glanced quickly over at Tara and then back at him, a gleam in her eyes. "For now, I'll let you keep your secrets." His eyebrows shot up in question. She spoke as if she already knew that he was there because of the pretty blonde behind the counter.

She stood up and sighed moments before a pair of teenagers walked through the door. "Enjoy your stay in Hidden Creek," she added as she walked back over to take the teens' orders.

He sat in the coffee shop until it grew too crowded and then made his way back out to his truck. Since it didn't appear that Tara was leaving the coffee shop any time soon, he made his way over to the hotel and got a room, showered, and changed into clean clothes. Then he headed back to the coffee shop to watch and wait, which, he had to admit, was what he did the majority of the time he worked.

In the past month, she'd given him the slip a few times before, so he was determined to keep his eyes on her this time.

Since Jess had shown such great interest in him and who his client was, he knew she was the type of woman that would look out for one of her workers, even a temporary one.

He didn't want to come across as a stalker, which meant he couldn't sit right in front of the coffee shop. Since it was a small town, he parked his truck down the street, just out of sight of the large windows of the shop.

A few hours later, at two in the afternoon, he watched Jess turn off the open sign in the window. A few moments later, the two women walked out together, chatting. Jess handed Tara a piece of paper, then quickly walked over to a small sedan and drove off. Tara stood in the parking lot, looking around the town.

He held his breath; afraid she would spot him parked down the street. But his windows were tinted very dark, and he relaxed when she climbed into her van. She probably didn't know what kind of car he drove. Plus, he doubted she had given him any more attention than she had anyone else. After all, she'd only seen him twice now.

Honestly, if it wasn't for the money, he would have lost interest in the job already. The pretty blonde was an anomaly. She didn't stay at hotels like most women he'd known would have done. Instead, she just parked the old white conversion van on the side of the road whenever she got tired. It had been one of the reasons it had been very difficult for him to find her.

He'd figured that when she needed money, she stopped somewhere and worked, usually at a coffee shop or a diner.

In the past month, she'd held four such jobs, each usually lasting only a few days, which is why it had been almost impossible to catch up to her. He figured she was working for gas and food money.

The question that kept running through his mind was why she was constantly on the move. Did she know he was tailing her?

Where was she heading to? What was the purpose? Why not stay in one place? Who was she running from?

His client hadn't given him much information on Tara. Only a grainy picture of the blonde, the make and model of her van, and where she'd been a little over a month ago. When he'd arrived, he'd missed her by three days, and he'd been following her breadcrumbs ever since.

He wasn't sure why someone was paying him to watch her in the first place. She didn't seem special in any way. Sure, she was pretty. Her long blonde hair helped her stand out from the crowd, that and her sea green eyes. Especially now that he'd seen them up close instead of through the zoom lens on his camera. Up close, he'd gotten the full effect of the sexy color.

She was taller than most women at five-ten. Since he'd seen her in shorts earlier that day, he knew most of that height was sexy, toned, tan legs that seemed to go on forever.

The other thing that made her stand out was how skinny she was. It was obvious that she'd skipped a few meals. Meals, he thought, that she couldn't afford to miss.

No matter the reason that someone wanted Tara Dawson, he believed she was a good person. Which is more than he could say for the last dozen or so people he'd tailed.

Most of his jobs were catching cheating spouses or tracking down insurance fraud. This job had been out of his normal spectrum. Still, when he'd been offered triple his normal fee, he'd jumped at the chance.

After all, it wasn't as if he was going to kidnap the woman. All he had to do was watch her for a while and then convince her to meet with his client. If she refused, he was to update his client on her whereabouts so that they could come to her.

Now, as he followed her van down a bumpy lane, he started to wonder if she was just looking for a place to park for the evening or if she was actually heading somewhere.

When she pulled into a very long driveway, he parked across the street and waited. She stopped her van next to a police cruiser and sat in the car, waiting.

The house had obviously been the centerpiece for a plantation back in the day. It was a massive three-story white building and was bigger than any home he'd seen in town so far. The yard was well maintained, with a row of huge oak trees lining the long driveway. There wasn't a blade of grass out of order. Even in the fall weather, the flowers in front of the wide porch were still in full bloom.

He watched the building and Tara's van closely.

Less than a minute later, he glanced in the rearview mirror and saw Jess's car heading up the road, directly towards him. He thought about gunning the truck and heading out of there, but the only place to go was down the long driveway. There was a smaller house to the left with a short driveway, but something told him it was too late.

Jess stopped next to his truck and rolled down her window. He did the same. He tried to think of an excuse for why he would be there but came up blank.

Then he realized that Jess was smiling at him.

"Ready to join the party?" she asked easily. Not giving him a chance to answer, she nodded her head. "Follow me." She rolled up her window, giving him no choice but to follow her down the long driveway.

He parked next to Tara's van and climbed out of the truck.

"What's he doing here?" Tara asked Jess.

Jess just laughed and grabbed a paper bag from her back seat.

"Now that everyone's here, let's head inside. It's going to rain soon," she said without looking up at the sky.

As if her words had commanded the weather, a drop of water hit him on the cheek.

Tara's green eyes narrowed at him, then she quickly motioned for him to follow Jess up the wide porch steps. He knew better than to try and act chivalrous now and moved so Tara could follow him under the cover of the porch just as the rain started falling even harder.

There were swings, chairs, and even a small firepit on the wide porch. Potted flowers of all colors lined the steps and sitting area or hung from hooks overhead. The place looked well lived in, enjoyed, like home.

A wave of jealousy hit him and he quickly pushed it aside. He wasn't the kind of person that settled down.

His upbringing had him stepping aside so Tara could follow Jess inside. He noticed that the woman hadn't knocked or unlocked the front door, making him curious if this was her place or if she was expected. There were four other cars out front, including the cruiser.

"We're here," Jess called out as she set the paper bag down on a table just inside the doorway.

The stocky one-year-old boy from earlier that morning came wobbling into the foyer, followed by a black-and-white border collie. Jess bent down and grabbed up the boy and rained kisses over his face while telling him how much she'd missed him.

The dog took a moment to sniff both him and Tara, then turned and went back the way it had come in.

He took a moment to assess the home, much like Tara was doing. A beautiful winding staircase sat just inside the glass front doors. Small tables filled with flowers sat on either side.

To the left was a massive living room with an old iron stove fireplace that he assumed would heat up the entire main floor when lit.

The furniture was new. He'd expected it to be older, like in an old movie, but instead, two warm leather sofas sat facing one another with a chair at the end and a long coffee table in the middle. A massive flat screen television hung on the wall just to the left of the fireplace, as if it was an afterthought to the space.

He could see a dining room down a short hallway and assumed the kitchen was just beyond that room.

A raven-haired woman with a small pink bundle in her arms followed the boy into the room.

"Good, we're all out back on the porch," the woman said, her eyes scanning over both Tara and him. Instead of being shocked about two newcomers in her house, she smiled warmly. "Welcome to our home. I'm sure Jess has left both of you wondering… well, everything. Come on back and you'll get some answers." She turned and walked back down the hallway.

Jess shifted her son and reached for the bag, but he beat her to it.

"I'll get this." He motioned for her to lead the way.

"This way," Jess said easily.

This time, he didn't wait for Tara's invitation. He followed Jess and felt Tara following behind him.

He was very curious to find out who these people were and why Tara was so willing to meet with them. Was this her final destination? Had she been traveling here all along?

The furniture in the dining room was older than the living room. A massive table with eight old high-back chairs sat in the center over a dark red rug that had probably been in the home since its construction. It was in good enough condition, but still, he could see the wear in the threads.

They passed through the kitchen and it too had been updated. Recently, apparently. Everything was new, modern, and very stylish.

A small door led to the back and a closed-in porch.

Here, there were nine other adults besides Jess and them. The cop from earlier stood up and planted a kiss on Jess's cheek and took their wiggly son from her arms.

The raven-haired woman sat down next to a man he assumed was her husband. The dog sat at the man's feet as if she owned him. The man next to him could easily be a brother to the first two men. He sat next to a pretty blonde woman who was obviously pregnant. Not quite ready to pop, but there was no doubt she was with child.

Across the large coffee table sat a man easily as muscular as he was. The man had his arm thrown over the shoulders of a redhead who was sipping tea. The last two people included a nerdy man with dark hair and glasses and a pretty brunette with hints of red in her hair, who was looking at Tara as if she'd seen a ghost.

"I know you," the woman said, and he felt Tara stiffen beside him.

CHAPTER 3

"You do?" Tara asked the brunette woman while her heart jumped in her chest.

"Don't I?" The woman narrowed her eyes at her, as if she was trying to place her.

"I don't think so," Tara answered, taking a step back.

Thankfully, Jess spoke up at that moment.

"Everyone, this is Tara and Colt, the two people I was telling you about." She waved towards them. "This is Xtina." She motioned to the raven-haired woman, and Tara instantly recognized her from the news article. "Her husband, Mike, and their daughter, Harper, who is two weeks old today." Jess smiled down at the baby. "This is Mike's twin, Ethan, and his wife, Brea, who is six months pregnant." She motioned to the man and the blonde next to him. "Over here we have Joe and Liz"—she motioned to the muscular man and the woman sitting beside him— "and Mason and Joleen, the newest members of the gang. Well, besides you two. Oh, and last but by far my favorite, my husband, Jacob, and our son, Reed."

Several greetings were tossed around. She recognized a few of the other faces around the room from the articles she'd found about the small town and its goings-on. Her eyes moved back to the brunette who had been introduced as Joleen. The woman did look familiar, but she couldn't place where she'd seen her before.

"Please sit." Xtina motioned towards the two empty chairs. "Would you like some tea?"

"Yes, please," Tara answered as she took a seat.

"Thanks," Colt said, and he moved over and sat next to her while Brea poured them each a glass of iced tea. She didn't know what Colt was doing there and since Jess hadn't answered her earlier, she was under the assumption that she'd invited him. After all, they'd spent some time talking to one another in the coffee shop.

Had they known one another before now? Something told her they hadn't. After all, Jess had just introduced him to all her friends.

"First things first," Xtina said, leaning forward and holding out her hands towards Tara. "If I may?" She motioned to her hands. Instantly, Tara knew what she was asking. After all, wasn't this why she was here in the first place, to get answers?

Tara hesitated for a split second, then she reached out and laid her hands in Xtina's.

The woman's green eyes shifted, changed color, until they were almost glowing.

"You are... something," Xtina said with a sigh and then quickly dropped Tara's hands and leaned back. "Wow." She shook her head. "I have never felt so much power." Xtina's eyes moved around the room. "Even with all of us"—her eyes landed on her again— "we don't have a drop in the bucket compared to the amount you have." She frowned. "I haven't felt this much power since..."

"Power?" Tara asked, feeling her palms start to sweat.

"What are you?" Xtina asked as her eyes ran over her.

Tara glanced around the room and noticed that everyone, including Colt, was watching her.

"I…" She shook her head. "I don't know."

"Let me try," Jess said easily, then she bent down, pulled out a book, and held her hands over the old leather binding. "I am Hecate, open," Jess said loudly. A blinding white light shot from the book and then the pages opened up and glowed white.

"What the…" Colt jumped to his feet.

"Sorry," Jess said, holding her hands up as if trying to calm a scared animal. "I should have… I'm a witch," she said quickly, opening her palm as a small flame lit in her hand and just as quickly disappeared. "A good one," she added with a smile. "Xtina's… well, Xtina." She chuckled. "She has the power of sight. Mike senses danger. My husband can control people when he locks eyes with them, as well as some other cool tricks." She winked at Jacob, who was holding a sleepy Reed. "Brea can teleport, Ethan heals, Joe is speedy, Liz is an oracle, and Joleen is a demi-god and can control time and space. Oh, and…"—Jess snapped her fingers— "Mason is a super nerd." Everyone chuckled.

"I believe the word you were looking for is super genius." The man turned to her. "I'm a super genius," he told Colt and Tara with a smile.

The room was silent for a moment. "You expect us to believe…" Colt waved his hands towards everyone.

Jess sighed and held out her hand. While they both watched, the pitcher of tea drifted into her hand, and she poured some more tea into her glass.

"Like *Bewitched*," Colt said under his breath as he slowly sat back down.

"Yes." Jess smiled at him. "I knew I'd like you."

Tara sat there, silent, while Colt continued to ask questions of the group. Brea stood up, disappeared, and then came back out of the back door with a tray of crackers and cheese, acting as if it was the most normal thing in the world.

Then it was Joe's turn. He stepped out the back door and disappeared in a streak and was back before she could blink, holding a case of beers in his hands. "They're cold." He held them up and stepped back inside.

Like Jess and Jacob, the rest of them had normal jobs. Mike and Ethan ran an online security business. Brea worked for the local paper, which is where all the stories Tara had read about the gang had come from. Joe owned and ran the local liquor store—hence, the beers. And Liz owned the veterinary clinic next door. Mason was a scientist and worked for an online college, while Joleen had recently become the manager for the local grocery store.

She listened while Colt explained that he also worked in security, like Mike and Ethan, but instead of cybersecurity, he was more of a private investigator. She didn't know why, but that thought made her very uncomfortable.

Finally, Colt's questions slowed down. Then he and everyone else in the room turned back to her.

"So, at this point, we just need to determine where you fit in to all this," Xtina said, looking at both her and Colt.

She glanced over at the man whom she'd only seen twice before this meeting.

"I don't know," Colt answered with a shrug. "I don't think I have any powers," he said easily. "None that I know of, anyway."

Xtina held out her hands for him, and Tara noticed him hesitate before laying his hands into hers.

She held her breath, waiting for Xtina's assessment of the man. Somehow, it mattered to her what these people thought of him. She didn't even know the man, yet she was invested. She felt a pull towards him.

When he sat next to her, it was as if she'd felt him near

her before. As if she'd known him her entire life. She couldn't quite put a finger on it, but she felt like she knew him.

"You have a good heart," Xtina said after she dropped her hands. "Intelligent and loyal. Those hold power you'll need in the coming weeks." Then she slumped back in her chair.

"You okay?" Jess asked Xtina.

"Yes, just... tired. I think I'm going to take Harper upstairs, feed her, and enjoy a new mother's nap with my little one." Xtina stood up, gently took the baby from Mike's hands, and walked out.

"It's our turn," Jess said to Tara. She pulled out the book again and glanced through the glowing pages.

"What is that?" Colt asked.

"My great-grandmother's book," Jess answered, without looking up. Suddenly, she set the book down on the table and glanced up at Tara. "I'll need something from you."

Tara frowned. "What?"

Jess smiled. "Nothing big, just a..." She leaned over and touched Tara's braided hair. "One strand ought to do it."

Her first inclination was to deny the request. After all, she'd just watched Jess hold fire in her hands and make things float about. But then she remembered that she'd sought them out. If she wanted answers, she was going to have to put herself out there. Reaching up, she took hold of her braid and pulled out the band holding back her thick hair. She handed over one of the strands of hairs that came loose.

Jess set the strand of hair in the book and then shut it.

"Is that it?" Tara asked.

"No, I won't know anything until after the next full moon," Jess said with a shrug. "Until then, you've got a job and, if you want, a place to park your van." She motioned to the driveway. "Xtina and Mike even have electric and plumbing hookups by the barn."

"You're welcome to use them," Mike chimed in. "That is, if you want to stick around."

Tara glanced around the table at all the faces, then landed on Colt and felt her heart jump in her chest. Did she want to stick around? Something about the man felt dangerous, but familiar.

"You haven't told us about you yet," Liz said with a smile, interrupting the silence.

"Me?" Tara said, swallowing.

Instead of answering, Liz nodded, the slight movement almost a sigh, as if she was telling her to get on with it.

"I…" She felt nervous for some reason. She could continue hiding or show this group of people what she could do. Hadn't she come here just for that reason?

Making up her mind, she stood up and glanced around the room. She spotted an old upright piano in the corner of the room and walked over to it. Turning to look at the faces of the people watching her, she realized that if she showed them, there wouldn't be any going back. She'd never exposed herself in such a way before, but she was tired of running. Tired of hiding who she was.

She bent down and picked up the corner of the piano and lifted it until the massive thing was above her head. She heard the gasps, then the claps, as she set it back down on the ground just as easily as she'd lifted it.

"Wow," Jess said. "Okay, that is pretty cool. Super strength."

"Is that all?" Liz asked, again with the slight smile. Tara narrowed her eyes at the woman. "I am an oracle," she reminded Tara. "I'm the one…" Jess cleared her throat, causing Liz to glance over at her and nod. "Right, Jess and I saw your arrival in town."

Tara glanced over at Colt, who was watching her closely.

She'd always believed that if she ever exposed her…

talents, that she'd be an outcast. Shunned. Instead, Colt was looking at her as if she was the most beautiful thing in the world.

Like she was something he craved.

Walking over, she opened the back screen porch and stepped outside, much like Joe had done earlier.

Instead of disappearing in a flash, she rose up and hovered almost five feet above the well-manicured grass.

"You can fly!" Jess squealed with excitement.

Feeling mentally drained, she set back down on the ground and nodded. "For short bursts," she admitted as she stepped back through the door. The power seemed to come and go. Sometimes she was stronger, other times not so much.

Everyone was looking at her as if she'd just won the lottery. Everyone except Colt, who was now frowning.

She didn't know why it hit her so hard, seeing that disapproval on his face. But shortly after that, she excused herself to the bathroom.

Taking her time, she washed her face, cooled the skin on the back of her neck, and tried to control the urge to disappear once more. When she stepped outside, Colt was standing in the hallway, waiting for her.

"Who else knows?" he asked her in a serious tone.

"Knows?" She shook her head.

"What you can do," he supplied.

"N-no one." She thought back to the times she'd slipped up over the years but bit her tongue. "No one," she said again. "Why?"

He glanced back down the hallway, where they could hear the group laughing at something. Then he took her hand and pulled her into a small office.

When he shut the door behind them, she stiffened.

"Where's your family?" he asked, his eyes searching hers.

"I… don't have any." She felt her entire body tense. "Why?" She frowned, not understanding why it mattered so much to him.

"You have to have someone in your past that's looking for you," he said more to himself than to her.

"No." She shook her head. "No one." She felt her stomach roll at that thought.

He swiped his hand through his short dark hair as he started to pace the small space. God, the man could move. She lost track of everything else just watching his muscles bunch as he crossed his arms over his chest and considered her.

"What the hell am I supposed to do now?" he asked her.

"About?" she asked, not really understanding what he was talking about.

"You."

Facts were facts. How was he supposed to spy on someone so... special? It was obvious to him now that Tara was an asset. Someone with such great power could be used. Controlled. Studied.

Whoever his client was, they obviously wanted to exploit her. The question now was whether he was going to allow it?

He turned back to Tara and watched the look of concern flood her eyes as he assessed her.

There was no doubt that she was attractive. Sexy as hell, actually.

Seeing her lift that piano like it weighed no more than a feather had been, disturbingly, a huge turn-on. But watching her fly. That had just been downright hot.

He'd never witnessed anything like it before in his life. Well, okay, he'd just watched Jess and Joe do some pretty cool tricks too.

"Is there anything else you can do?" he asked her as he moved closer. He couldn't help himself, he wanted to be next to her. To smell her soft sexy perfume, to see those green eyes of hers close up once more.

He had a quick thought about watching them change colors as he kissed her. Seeing how they'd shift and go dreamy when he entered her.

As if she could read his mind, her breath hitched, and she sucked in her bottom lip, biting it softly between her teeth. The move had him holding in a groan.

He hadn't realized that his hand had moved up to her shoulder until she glanced down at it. He dropped it and took a step back.

"No," she said, shaking her head and avoiding his eyes.

He'd worked long enough in the field to know when someone was lying to him. Whatever other powers she held, she wanted to keep them to herself for now.

He turned around and thought about the consequences of turning her in to the person who was paying him. Maybe he was jumping to conclusions too quickly? After all, he hadn't checked in with his client in the last few days. He hadn't told them that he'd found her again. What could it hurt to stall?

"Why? Why does it matter to you?" she asked him.

He glanced towards the doors when another burst of laughter sounded. "No reason." He walked over to open the door. "We'd better get back out there."

When Tara passed him this time, he heard her breath catch.

"What?" he asked softly.

She turned her face towards him. "Who are you?" she asked quietly.

"I told—" He stopped when she shook her head.

"You told them what you wanted them to hear." Her eyes narrowed at him. "Who are you?"

"Colt," he answered, unsure of what she was asking.

Her eyes ran over his face and locked with his, then she did something that shocked him. She reached up and ran a finger over his chin.

Thoughts of bending his head down and kissing her filled his mind. What would she taste like? How would her soft lips feel under his? Would she be full of passion, like he assumed?

As if she'd broken from a spell, she gasped, dropped her hand, and walked out of the room quickly. He followed her back out onto the covered porch and listened as the group continued to chat.

He had more questions but he didn't want to come across as too nosy. Instead, he sat and watched the couples interact. Almost an hour after disappearing upstairs with her baby, Xtina returned downstairs to be filled in on the amazing things Tara could do.

Which of course was followed by requests for another show. This time when the piano was lifted, he was prepared, as he was when her feet lifted off the ground. What he hadn't seen the first time he noticed now. The show seemed to drain Tara, making her look tired. When she sat back down beside him, she drank some tea and had some crackers and cheese and began to look better.

She didn't mention the drain to the others, and he figured he would keep that information to himself as well. He was happy when Xtina asked Tara if there was anything else she could do.

Tara glanced at him before shrugging.

"I haven't really explored too much more," she answered.

"Why not?" Mike asked.

"Afraid?" Joe asked. Then he chuckled. "I know that when I started using my gift a little more, I realized how careful I had to be. Once, I was almost caught on a surveillance camera. Try explaining to the government why you decided to run across the border for a case of tequila."

"You did not." Liz slapped him playfully.

Joe chuckled and rolled his eyes. "I may or may not have."

"Using my abilities drains me," Xtina said. "Does that happen with you?" she asked Tara.

"I—" Tara started, but then Jess jumped in.

"Sure it does. I mean, look at her. She's what? Thirty pounds underweight?" Jess shook her head.

Tara seemed to fall back against the chair, shrinking in front of everyone.

"Speaking of food," Ethan broke in, "it's about time we put those steaks on the grill. How about you help us out, Colt?"

"Sure." Colt stood up, eager to help. It had been years since he'd grilled out, though he had always enjoyed it. Actually, cooking was sort of his thing. He found the task of making a meal more soothing than lifting weights.

As he followed the brothers into the kitchen to help prepare the food, he realized just how alike the two men were.

"Ex-military?" he asked after only two minutes alone with them.

"Yup," Mike answered then narrowed his eyes at him. "Army?"

Colt nodded. "Special ops. You?" He could tell both men had served.

"Yeah. Ethan was in longer than I was," Mike answered. "I retired and went into law, then started the cybersecurity business after an injury."

"You?" he asked Ethan.

"Special Forces," Ethan answered as he set the tray of steaks down on the counter. "Medical discharge last year. Now I help him out." He motioned to his brother.

"Jacob is…" He let the question hang in the air.

"Our older brother we didn't know we had until about two years ago," Mike answered.

"But he's family now," Ethan added. "So, are you a good cook?"

Colt chuckled. "I was the best in my troop."

"Oh!" both men said at the same time, smiling.

"Looks like we got us a new chef." Ethan handed him the spatula. "You take the lead."

"Don't like to cook?" he asked the brothers.

"We drew the short straws tonight," Mike offered.

For the next few minutes, the three of them worked together in the kitchen, marinading the steaks, making a potato salad, and oiling up some fresh vegetables for the grill.

"Do the ten of you hang out all the time?" he asked as he followed them out back towards the grill, holding a tray of steaks.

"No, just when we're called in for a meeting," Ethan answered. "Mike and I, our wives, and Jacob and Jess meet at least three times a week. But everyone else, only when we're called in."

"So, how did the gang come together?" he asked as he started heating up the grill.

While he cooked, Mike and Ethan sat across the outdoor bar area and told him the story of how everyone met.

He listened as they explained how the group had fought off Thanatos, the god of death.

Then they moved on to tell the story of how they had fought more gods a little over a year later and Liz had sent Aither, Nyx, and Erebus back to Tartarus for their eternal slumber.

"Don't forget Hypnos," Ethan broke into the story. "He helped Liz out a little," he added with a shrug.

"Right." Colt nodded. Okay, so the power thing was pretty cool, but now he was beginning to think the men were just straight-up nuts. He'd studied enough Greek mythology in high school to know the characters they spoke of. He didn't remember every detail about each god, but at least he wasn't at a complete loss.

"After that, Joleen and Mason came into town. Well, Joleen had always been in town, but then we had to send Thanatos away again. This time for good," Mike said.

"We locked him up in a deep chasm on the moon along with Jess's mother," Ethan added.

"Okay," he said slowly, glancing towards the back of the house.

Then suddenly, both men started laughing.

"You were joking?" He felt a sliver of relief.

"No, it's just..." Mike shook his head. "I never really thought of just how crazy it would sound to an outsider." He shook his head.

"Then again, we've never really told any outsiders before," Ethan added.

Just then, Jacob came strolling over, carrying a case of beer. "Compliments of Joe." He held them up. "They're cold."

Colt took a beer and sipped while he flipped the steaks.

"Did you catch him up on everything? I think Tara thinks we're all nuts," Jacob said, nodding back towards the house.

"I think Colt believes it too," Mike said with a smile. "No one really believes it until you live through it. I know it took me a while to believe it after it happened. And I was there and saw it."

"Yeah." Jacob ran his hands through his hair. "Still can't believe it all sometimes myself. Then Jess will cause something to float or she'll disappear and reappear with something and—bam—I realize just how possible it all is."

"Not to mention your wife saw them coming." Mike motioned towards him.

The three men looked at him.

"Do you think it's true what Liz said..." Ethan started, only to get a jab in the ribs from Mike.

"Later," Mike said under his breath.

"Looks like the food's about done," Jacob interjected quickly.

The conversation turned to Mike and Ethan's business. Thankfully. Here, at least, he knew that the men had some sanity.

While they talked about their new deal with Fanatics, they carried the food inside. The large table in the dining room had been set and everyone was gathered around, waiting for the food.

Wine had replaced the beer as the food was passed around. Once again, he sat next to Tara. He was slightly surprised at how much more relaxed she seemed than before.

If anything, he was a little more cautious himself. All the talk of fighting off gods didn't really sit well with him.

Had the group suffered from a combined hallucination or had something really happened to them? At any rate, by the time the food was gone, he was pretty sure that everyone at the table, minus him and Tara, truly believed that gods were real and that they had indeed saved the planet from them multiple times in the past few years.

Shortly after sunset, Xtina excused herself and the baby once more, telling everyone goodnight. Then Jess and Jacob mentioned they had early mornings, and Jess turned to Tara.

"We open at five. See you there." It wasn't a question, but a statement. He was thankful when Tara smiled and nodded in agreement. He could see the eagerness in her eyes and the truth that she was really sticking around town. At least for now.

Thankfully, he knew that she wouldn't be taking off in the middle of the night on him.

Mike walked them out front as everyone else was leaving.

"If you want, you're welcome to park the van where it is. We do have a guest room, but Xtina thinks you won't take us up on our offer to stay in it," Mike said.

"She's right." Tara nodded. "I'm more comfortable in my own place. It may be tiny, but it's all mine." She smiled. "Thank you. I will, however, agree to hook up to your water and power, if it's okay with you."

"Sure is. I had the connections installed a few months back for my parents, who just bought a huge RV. But they have decided to travel since my dad likes the open road." He rolled his eyes. "They are just by the barn. It's over here." Mike walked towards the other building to the right.

Since he figured he could help, he followed along. Besides, he was kind of curious to see what the inside of her van looked like. Did she have a shower? A toilet? In the last month he'd never seen her check into a hotel to shower. She always came out of the van looking fresh and clean, which led him to believe there was more room on the inside than it seemed.

Mike and he stood back as she backed her van up next to the garage and opened the sliding door. To his surprise, there was not only a shower area with a toilet inside, but a full-blown kitchen, a small dining space, and a king-sized bed.

"Wow," Mike said, looking inside. "It's like a tiny home on wheels," he joked.

"Thanks. I built most of it out myself." Tara hooked up the power and water connections. "It had some parts when I bought it, but the rest I upgraded."

He had to admit, he was more than a little impressed.

"You... live in this full time?" Mike asked.

"Yes," she answered with a smile. "I guess you can say I like the open road too."

"Not that I don't enjoy a good trip, but..." He glanced back at the big house and smiled. "I've got a few things here worth sticking around for."

Tara smiled. "Your daughter is charming."

"She will be." Mike chuckled. "When she does more than

sleep, eat, and poop." Mike reached out his hand. "Well, I'd better get inside and see to my women." Colt shook his hand. "Goodnight." He gave Tara a nod and then strolled back towards the house.

"They're very trusting," Tara said, mostly to herself.

"They're all insane," he added with a shake of his head.

CHAPTER 5

Tara felt her entire body tense.

"Why? Because they let a stranger stay on their land?" she asked.

"No." Colt shook his head. "Because they…" He shrugged. "They did tell you the whole story about fighting off gods, right?"

She relaxed slightly and took a deep breath of the sultry autumn air. She'd spent most of her life in California and in the northern states. She'd never been somewhere where at ten o'clock at night it was still so warm outside. Not to mention all the humidity. She found she kind of liked it.

At least she wouldn't have to run the space heater in her van tonight. Actually, she might even open the windows and let some of the scent of the flowers planted around the garage soothe her to sleep.

"Yeah." She waved him off and started walking around her van to pull out the folding chair that she used to enjoy the outdoors. She had two of them and since Colt didn't show any signs of leaving soon, she pulled them both out.

"That doesn't concern you?" he asked as he helped her set them up.

"No." She shook her head and reached inside to grab a couple of cold sodas from her fridge. She handed him one and sat down and enjoyed the view of the fireflies playing over the dark field beyond the barn. "You're forgetting, I just showed everyone I could lift a piano and fly," she added dryly, even though she was still reeling inside from letting out her secrets to strangers. But part of her trusted that they wouldn't call in the government agents and have her hauled away. She hoped. "Besides, over the past years I've learned not to look a gift horse in the mouth." She smiled. "Or a free spot to park and stay with hookups."

He sat next to her and sipped his soda. "Right." He frowned into the darkness.

She could tell he was debating asking her something.

"What?" she asked after a moment. When he looked at her, she shrugged. "It's obvious you want to ask me something." She waved her hand. "Shoot. It's not like I didn't just open myself up completely in there already."

"Right." He shifted in the chair, then set down his drink on the ground next to the chair. "Have you always had the abilities?"

"No," she answered quickly.

"When did they come to you?"

"Shortly after my sixteenth birthday," she answered easily, trying to push aside the memoires of her childhood, of everything she'd lost. "Who did you come in town to work for?" she asked, turning the tables on the questioning.

He was silent for a while before answering. "I didn't come to town to work for someone in Hidden Creek, specifically."

She narrowed her eyes at him. "You're here for me, aren't you?" She'd thought about it since the moment he'd mentioned what he did for a living. Her gut had told her he was after her the instant he'd mentioned that he found people, spied on people. Something just hadn't sat right. Besides, it was too much of a coincidence to run into him in the gas station that morning and then see him at the coffee shop more than a hundred miles away.

Instead of answering, he stood up and walked over to the wood fence a few feet away under a dim light that hung on the corner of the garage.

Moths danced in the beam of the floodlight, and the crickets' chirps were almost deafening. She moved to stand next to him.

"Why me? I'm nobody," she asked.

He turned to her. "I thought that at first." His eyes ran over her. "Then you lifted a piano like it was a feather." He sighed. "Oh, yeah, and flew."

She nodded. "Okay, who is your client, then? Someone from my past? I mean, I'm careful not to mess up, but I'm not perfect," she admitted as fear spiked through her. Was he going to turn her in? Part of her was screaming to pack up and drive away at that very moment. Still, the way he was looking at her, the kindness and concern she saw in his eyes, had her leaning against the fence and watching him.

"So someone else knows what you can do?" he asked her.

"No. I mean, I don't think so." She thought about it. About all the times she'd slipped up in the past. When she'd lifted something that would have been way too heavy for someone her size. Or the time she'd jumped a little too high to reach the top shelf in the store. Not to mention the time she'd poured hot liquid on her skin and walked away without even a red mark.

"Can you think of anyone in particular?" he asked, as if he wasn't even sure who his client was himself.

Sighing, she shook her head. "Don't you even know who hired you?"

He glanced away and shrugged. "I have a name, but..." She chuckled and he turned back towards her. "What?" he asked, turning those sexy dark eyes towards her again.

"Don't you find people for a living? Surely you know who it is that hired you by now?"

He looked away again, and she felt weariness flood her.

"Can I have their name?" she asked.

His eyes narrowed, and he shook his head slowly. "Not... yet."

"Are you going to tell your client where I am?" she asked after a moment of silence.

He turned his entire body towards hers, and she realized just how close they were standing to one another. Her breath hitched while her heart pounded in her chest. Why did this all feel so familiar? While his eyes ran over her face, she waited, trying to figure him out.

"No," he finally answered. "Not yet. It's like you said, I find people. It's about time I found out who I'm working for and why. Then..." He dropped off and balled his hands into fists, as if he was trying to hold something back. "When and if I let my client know where you are, I'll let you know first," he said, shocking her. "That's a promise."

She felt her heart settle in her chest.

"Thank you," she said softly.

"I'll let you get some rest." He turned to go but stopped and looked back at her. "Something tells me you can do far more than you showed them." He motioned to the now dark house. "Just so you know, I plan on doing a lot more research into..."—he nodded towards the house again— "everyone. I'll let you know if I find anything you should be concerned about."

"Why?" she asked before he had a chance to walk away.

He flashed her a smile that made her knees go weak. "Call it intuition." He surprised her by lifting his hand and running a finger down her long hair. "Or maybe your powers extend to controlling others," he joked.

She smiled. "If I had that power, I wouldn't have to move around so much."

"Right." He nodded. "Goodnight." He turned and climbed into his truck, and she watched his taillights disappear down the long driveway.

She stood outside for a few moments, enjoying the peace and quiet, hearing only crickets. Glancing up at the sliver of the moon in the dark sky, she wrapped her arms around herself and felt a shiver race down her spine.

She might have been okay showing Xtina and her group some of her tricks, but there was one secret she doubted she could trust anyone with. Something so shocking about herself that she knew no one would ever understand.

She was going to be the reason everything disappeared. She'd seen it in her dreams more times than she could count. She would bring the darkness. The end of the world. Whatever was coming, she knew she had to prepare. Which is why she'd come to Hidden Creek. She needed help if anyone was going to survive the apocalypse she'd foreseen. But before she trusted them completely with the future, she wanted to make one-hundred percent sure she could trust them. Only then would she let them in on her visions.

The following morning, almost two hours after she clocked into her new job, Colt walked through the door of the Coffee Corner. It didn't surprise her when Jess had placed his order moments before he arrived, since the woman had been calling out people's orders all morning.

At first, she'd believed that they were regulars who came in at the same time each day or that Jess just knew everyone's schedules. But then one of the women had said she was in town on an unexpected errand, and still Jess had her order ready.

She figured it was part of Jess's powers and made a note to ask her about it when they were alone. Did all witches have the ability to see how everyone liked their coffee?

After Colt walked in, she stopped questioning Jess's abilities and just went with it.

She had to admit, it was nice working again. Keeping busy kept her mind from... things. Until Colt walked in. Then her mind was consumed with him. And it wasn't just worry about why someone had hired him to find her. Her main thoughts were about how damn sexy he looked in his worn jeans and tight T-shirt. The weather had turned in the middle of the night, but not even the light jacket he was wearing could hide how good he looked.

She'd slept with the windows open and had to shut them sometime after three when she'd woken chilled. She liked fall weather, but it was the first time she'd experienced colder weather in the south. Somehow, with all the moisture in the air, it made her feel even colder than being in two feet of snow and ice in Montana.

"Morning," Colt said as he stepped up to the counter.

"Morning," Jess had said cheerfully. "How did you sleep?"

"Fine." His eyes moved past Jess and landed on hers. "You?"

She knew the question was for her, but Jess answered cheerfully. "Like the dead." She chuckled. "Ever since Reed started sleeping all through the night, we get a full seven hours, uninterrupted. Tara has your coffee ready."

He frowned down at the cup, then his eyebrows shot up as he looked at Jess.

"It's a talent to know everyone's orders before they walk in," Jess said with a shrug. Then she turned to Tara. "Why don't you take a break? It's finally slowed down enough for you to enjoy your complimentary breakfast."

Jess set two massive cinnamon rolls on individual plates

and handed one to Colt and one to her. When Jess gave her a look that clearly said not to argue with her, she took the plate and made herself a cup of her favorite morning drink.

Since Jess was watching them, she followed Colt to a table and sat across from him.

"Something tells me you couldn't have gotten out of that if you'd tried," Colt said under his breath.

Tara chuckled. "I was thinking the same thing." Then she leaned closer to him. "Did you do your research?"

"I did." He took a bite of his cinnamon roll and his look showed that he was impressed with it, so she bit into her own and instantly agreed.

"And?" she asked.

"And so far, everyone is who they say they are. Xtina's real name is—"

"Christina," she supplied with a smile. "Yeah, I already knew that."

"Okay." He nodded and took another bite. "So you know what she went through a little over a year ago? Her parents' death and the kidnapping from the cult?"

"Yes." She nodded and said in a low tone, "The reason I'm in Hidden Creek is because of that article Brea wrote."

His eyebrows shot up again. "You came here... for them?"

She nodded and could tell that he was thinking about it. "Because of... everything last night?" he asked, glancing around. She nodded again as she took another bite of her roll.

He was silent for a while as they both enjoyed their food and coffee.

"Why?" he asked after a moment.

She looked deep into his brown eyes and figured there wasn't any use hiding anything more from him. At least not about this.

"I think they might have some answers as to where I came

from," she answered, figuring to keep the darker things for after breakfast.

"Before Seattle?"

She shook her head. "No," she said softly and watched as recognition of what she was admitting crossed his face.

CHAPTER 6

$\mathcal{C}$olt watched Tara's expression. At first, he thought she was joking, but then it all sank in. She honestly believed that she'd come from somewhere else. She believed she was an alien of some sorts.

Gods and aliens. In Georgia. What the hell had he stumbled onto?

Realization dawned on him as he remembered everything he'd witnessed.

No wonder someone was after her. What kind of person would he be if he turned her in to them now? He thought about what would happen if he did. What if he didn't? Would they still hunt her down?

This was his first big client, but that didn't temper his resolve to at least try to figure out why they wanted her. In the past three years, he'd made a decent enough living to keep him in the one-bedroom apartment just outside of Seattle where he had started this entire journey.

What had Tara been doing in Washington State to begin with?

"What do you mean where you came from? Like, from another planet? Like an alien?" he asked.

Tara shrugged slightly and glanced towards the door as a group of people stepped inside.

"I better get back."

"Sure," he agreed. "Later, I'd like to talk some more?"

"Sure, I get off work at…"

"Two," Jess called out.

Tara smiled. "Two."

"How about I swing by then?"

She glanced towards Jess, who was already taking the customers' orders. "I'll be here." She disappeared behind the counter, taking her empty plate and cup with her.

He finished eating and sipping his coffee and then headed back to the hotel. He needed to dig deeper into who his client was, but instead, he sat in his hotel room and tried to find anything else on Tara that he could.

The woman, it seemed, had no online presence. When he came up with a complete blank in the databases that he had access to, he pulled up a picture of her van and searched the license plate registration.

The registration was from Oregon, and a few months outdated. When he looked closer, he realized it was registered to a mailbox store address. The same address was on Tara's driver's license. Was that even legal?

He kept searching. The first job she'd held was in a small coffee shop in the Seattle area when she was seventeen. Before that, there was no record of her. Not even a high school diploma or birth certificate.

As far as he could tell, Tara Dawson had just… appeared one day.

What he'd found out last night about the rest of the Hidden Creek gang, as he was calling everyone who had been there last night, had been far more detailed than what he'd found on Tara.

Mike and Ethan were your standard run-of-the-mill ex-military types. Kind of like he was. They'd served their time and had either gotten out or had been injured. Mike had gone into law enforcement and then, upon getting shot by his partner, had retired and gone into private security.

The fact that he and Mike had that in common played heavily on his mind. If the guy could make it, then there was hope for him.

Ethan, on the other hand, had been injured in the line of duty and had gotten an honorable medical discharge. Then he'd moved to Hidden Creek and started working with his brother.

Jacob St. Clair. Now he was an anomaly. He was the adopted son of Ronny and Clair St. Clair. Ronny was the old law in the small town.

But last night, the brothers had told him that Jacob was their older brother. After doing a little more digging, Colt found an article written by Brea about how the brothers had found one another by chance. It went into detail about how Rusty and Susan Kincaid, Mike and Ethan's parents, had been forced to give up their first son when they'd still been in high school.

The grainy image of the three men and their parents assured him and anyone with eyes that they were indeed all related.

Joe Reed was no mystery. Everything the man had been or done was easily found in the Hidden Creek newspaper or the school archives online. He'd been a gym rat since hitting puberty and had taken over the local liquor store after his uncle's death. It was the only one within thirty miles of town, so its success was assured.

He had a younger sister, Amy, who was away at college in

Atlanta. His parents still lived in town and lived a pretty normal small-town life.

Mason Barrett was everything the scientist said he was last night. The man's credentials were almost as impressive as Stephen Hawking's.

Liz's and Joleen's backgrounds were straightforward, at least from what he could find on them.

But when he'd looked into the rest of the women, there were more entanglements.

Xtina's parents had been killed in a car accident and several members in a cult had been charged with the crime. After their leader had been killed by Mike on the night they'd kidnapped Xtina, the cult members had turned on one another, which had made charging them with the crime easy.

Jess's mother was MIA, but her father had recently moved back into town, as had Brea's father, who was now married to her aunt, Misty.

After scanning over his notes about the rest of the players, he figured he'd do more research on Tara to see if he could find anything new.

He spent so much time looking into her past that when it was time to go and meet her, he'd only spent a few moments looking into his client.

When he parked in front of the Coffee Corner, Jess and Tara were the only two people inside. He sat in the parking lot, watching the two women chatting. They looked comfortable around one another, like they were old friends. Was it possible? Had Tara really been here before?

No. Yesterday was proof of that. She hadn't known anyone else at Xtina and Mike's place.

He supposed Tara was so comfortable since she'd spent the last ten years hopping from one coffee shop to the next. Her people skills had to be good enough to keep her in work.

He watched as they walked out of the Coffee Corner.

Tara's eyes moved to his truck, and she waved easily in his direction. It was then that he noticed that her van wasn't in the parking lot. Most likely, Jess had picked her up that morning and had driven them both into work.

Jess climbed into her own car as Tara headed towards his truck. He was thankful that it appeared that she wanted him to take her back to her van.

"I hope it's okay," she said, opening his driver side door and climbing in. "Jess insisted that it would be okay with you if you took me back to my van after our chat."

"Sure." He smiled quickly, then frowned slightly when the sweet scent of coffee mixed with her perfume had his loins responding. "Where to?" he asked.

She shrugged and glanced around. "Jess mentioned this really great park just outside of town. We could go for a hike?" Tara suggested.

He glanced over at her. "Didn't you just stand on your feet for the past eight hours or so?"

She chuckled, the sound warm and sultry, making him instantly think of long lazy nights making slow love to her.

"I think I can handle a little walk. I need some fresh air anyway."

He pulled out of the parking lot and followed her directions to the park, all while trying not to think about fulfilling his desires.

When they climbed out of the truck in the state park's parking lot, he grabbed a couple of bottled waters from his supply in the back seat and handed her one.

"Thanks," she said and glanced around. "Are you up for this?"

This time he chuckled. "I usually hike twenty miles a weekend. I like to camp too," he added. "Course, what you've got going, with the van and all, is far better than my old one-person tent."

Her eyebrows shot up slightly. "It does have its benefits," she said as they started down the trail head. "Like a toilet, shower, and clean water. Not to mention my very own full kitchen and pillow-top mattress."

"Yeah, how does all of that fit in there?" he asked, curious. He'd seen it himself, but it was still hard to believe all of that fit in such a small space.

She shrugged. "Magic, I suppose. I bought it and built out the inside myself. I'd seen a few vans like it and wanted to make it my own."

"In Seattle?" he asked, glancing sideways at her.

"No, I bought the van in Seaside, Oregon, from a couple that had to get rid of it so they could buy their first house because she was pregnant with triplets," she responded with a hint of humor in her voice.

"Wow." He shook his head. "Going from two to five in one day."

She stopped in the pathway and looked at him. "Don't like kids?"

He smiled. "Love 'em." He thought about it for a moment. "But I'd like mine to be a little more spaced out. You know, get used to one of the little guys before being thrust headfirst into changing three sets of diapers."

She nodded and started walking again.

"Why travel so much?" he asked her after a few moments.

"Why not?" She shrugged.

"Family?" he asked, trying to keep the question casual. He hadn't found out anything about her family in his research.

"Nope," she answered.

This time he stopped her by placing a hand on her elbow lightly. She turned towards him.

"I'm sorry. Did they die?"

She took a deep breath and then looked around. They were surrounded by tall pine and oak trees. Even though it was fall, only the oak tree's leaves were orange and brown. Everything else was still vibrant green.

He listened as she thought about her answer, counting the calls from a mockingbird until finally she said, "I don't know."

"Did they take off on you like Jess's parents did?"

"Not… necessarily," she answered, and he could hear the pain in her voice. She took a deep breath and then stopped at the peak of a hill and sat on a large boulder. He sat next to her as she tucked her knees up to her chest. "It was my sixteenth birthday party," she started, as her eyes scanned the horizon of plush green and orange trees ahead of them. "I had the most perfect party arranged and all of my close friends had been invited. The moment I blew out the candles on the cake, everyone just…" She flipped her fingers into the air. "Disappeared. My entire world was gone in a heartbeat."

"Gone?" he asked, not really understanding.

She nodded and glanced over at him, and he watched a tear slip down her cheek. Reaching over, he gently brushed it away with his thumb.

"I'm sorry," he said, meaning it. He'd experienced loss in his own life, having lost his older sister and father to a drunk driver when he'd been in middle school.

Her breath hitched when he touched her, and she swayed towards him until they were so close, he could see her pupils dilate. Her tongue darted out, and she licked her bottom lip. He wondered what she would taste like, how soft her lips would feel under his.

He didn't remember moving. Didn't know if she'd been the one who'd leaned in and placed her lips over his. It didn't matter who had moved first after Tara's response to the kiss. Her body melted against his as her fingers tangled in his hair.

"I didn't mean to do that," she said as she rested her forehead against his chest. Then she chuckled. "It's the first time

I've told anyone about that day." She glanced up at him. "And it's been a while since I've wanted to be with someone."

He smiled. "What do you say we head back and grab some food? I was so busy doing research that I forgot to eat lunch."

She stood up suddenly. "I could eat," she agreed and they headed back down the trail.

"I'd love to hear the story of how you discovered you could fly and lift heavy things," he said as they made their way back to his truck.

She chuckled before starting. "Most of what I can do was discovered by accident."

He waited a heartbeat. "Kind of like Superman?"

She glanced over at him and rolled her eyes. "Men and their superheroes."

"What?" He stopped her. "You can't tell me you don't admire the man of steel?"

She smiled. "I'm more of a Wonder Woman kind of girl."

"She's hot too," he said, adding a shrug when Tara slapped him playfully on the shoulder. "What? I mean, what man wouldn't want a woman who can bend steel, take down Nazis, and fly." He realized what he was admitting the moment the words were and didn't care. "Hot," he added with a smile.

"Not everyone thinks the same way." Her smile slipped slightly. "Which is why I've spent the past ten years moving around a lot."

"What happened?" he asked when they reached the bend in the pathway.

She stopped and turned towards him. "I had started seeing this guy, Rob, after I found out about my strength. He wanted to videotape me showing off, and at first, I thought it was a fun thing to do. I was excited about pleasing him. Then he started planning and plotting. That's when he threatened to send the videos to the government, who would, according to him, hunt me down and dissect me, if I didn't start doing things."

"What kind of things?" he asked, already hating the guy.

"For starters, breaking into ATMs."

"Did you?"

She shook her head. "No, I took off instead."

"What happened to Rob?" he asked.

"He put the videos up on the internet where they were immediately labeled as fake. People just can't believe something like that really exists. Something like me," she said softly.

He reached over and took her hand and then pulled her into his arms. "From the looks of things last night, you're no longer alone." He felt his heart skip when she smiled.

CHAPTER 7

What was Tara supposed to do with Colt? She'd never had someone treat her like he did. Not only had he confessed that he thought her abilities were hot, but just the way he'd responded to her story about Rob had instantly told her that he was as disgusted by her ex as she had been.

Not to mention that kiss. She'd been close to power for years but had never felt it so strong before. The pull of attraction she felt towards Colt was as great as the force that had driven her from her home all those years ago.

"Hey, I have a strange idea," he said, taking a slight step back from her.

Thoughts of getting him naked and running her hands over the muscles she could see through his T-shirt had her body reacting quickly.

"Okay," she practically purred.

His eyes moved to her lips briefly, but then he took another step back.

"Since it appears that this park isn't that crowded, how

about you give me another sample of what you can do?" he asked, and her mind snapped to attention.

"Don't trust your own eyes?" she asked.

"Let's just say I wasn't really paying close enough attention." His sly smile had her laughing.

"You just think it's hot," she teased.

"Hell, yes, but…" His smile slipped slightly. "Humor me?" he asked.

She shrugged and, after glancing around to ensure that they were alone on the pathway, she lifted a giant log that had fallen on the side of the path. When the dirt and bugs dropped to the ground, she set it back down and stood back as he walked over to it. She smirked when he bent down and tried to lift the massive thing.

"Okay, so it wasn't a trick," he said with a slight frown.

Her eyebrows shot up. "You thought…" She shook her head.

"What? You can't blame me. I mean, I couldn't have tried to pick up the piano with a room full of people watching. I would have…" He shook his head.

"Looked weak if you couldn't pick it up?" she suggested, getting a chuckle from him.

"Hell, yes, but that's not the point." He nodded. "You know, you could have had wires on," he said with a smirk.

"I'll do one better." She walked up to him, wrapped her arms around him, and watched as his eyes moved to her lips again. This time, when she pressed her lips to his, she waited until she felt him lose himself in the kiss before lifting off the ground.

She felt the moment he realized what she'd done. His arms wrapped around her tighter as he pulled away from the kiss.

"What!" he said, glancing down. The pathway was now more than fifteen feet below them. They were still deep under the cover of the trees, but now instead of the leaves being below them, they were among them.

The branches of a large oak that sat by the trail were now easily within arm's reach.

"Whoa," he said, laughing. She smiled. "I figure this was an easier way of convincing you." She started drifting back down towards the trail.

"How do you control it?" he asked as their feet touched the ground.

"I just… think it," she said with a shrug.

"That simple?" He dropped his hands away from her and glanced back up to where they had just been.

"Yes," she said, following his gaze. "It's a good thing I'm not afraid of heights."

"So, you what? Just lifted me or did you cause me to fly too?" he asked, looking a little put off.

She couldn't help it, she laughed. "I didn't mean to damage your male ego," she said when she was done.

He chuckled. "Honey, for a trip like that, you can damage me anytime." He reached over and easily took her hand again. "Just next time, give me a little warning."

She smiled the entire way back down the trail. No man had ever been so… casual about her gifts before, so accepting. Then again, after the fiasco with Rob, she'd kept what she could do to herself.

The moment she'd seen the video of herself lifting heavy weights at the gym that Rob had put online, she'd felt sick to her stomach. She was sure that at any moment, government agents were going to find her and take her away to some secret lab. After all, she knew from that moment on that she wasn't normal. Couldn't be. Not with all the other things she could do. The things she wasn't ready to tell anyone else about just yet.

"How about the pizza joint in town?" he asked her.

"Sure, sounds good." She watched the scenery go by outside the truck window. "What about you?" She glanced over at him. "You've done your research and found out what there is to know about me, so how about you shed some light on yourself?"

"Sure," he said with a shrug. "I was born the second son in a family of three. My oldest brother Colin, named after my father, runs the family business back in Seattle."

"Which is?" she asked.

"A bakery," he said with a smile.

"Tell me you can bake," she said.

He chuckled. "I don't mean to brag, but my cinnamon rolls would put Jess's to shame."

"Okay." She nodded. "Of course, you'll have to prove it to me."

He chuckled. "I accept the challenge."

"What about Colin Sr.?" she asked.

His smile instantly fell away. "Died when I was thirteen in a car accident, along with my sister, Carrie."

"I'm so sorry." She reached out to touch his hand.

"Dad had just dropped me off at school and was taking Carrie out to the high school when a young mother with three kids of her own plowed right into them. Her blood alcohol was almost twice the legal limit. She and her children survived. My sister and dad didn't."

She was silent for a moment. Now she knew why he had been so understanding when she'd mentioned the loss of her family. Half of his had been taken from him as well.

"My mom and brother took over the bakery. After I graduated, I enlisted in the army. I spent a few years traveling the world, shooting at things." He shrugged. "Then I came back and started this as a side gig while I helped out my family," he finished as he parked in front of the pizzeria.

"You followed me from Seattle?" she asked with a frown.

She'd moved around so much in the past few months, she had to think back to when she'd ended back up in Seattle. Thinking back, she realized it had been a little over a month ago.

"Yeah." He nodded and started to get out.

"Colt, that was over a month ago." She shook her head, thinking about all of the places she'd been. Everything she'd done since she'd left the state.

He shrugged. "My client was insistent that I not lose track of you."

"Why?" She frowned. "I mean, I get it if they happened to see me fly." She waved her hand in a fluttering motion. "Or lift something heavy. Though I've been very careful not to do any of that in a public setting. But why pay you whatever it is they are paying you to follow me across the country?"

He shrugged. "I don't argue with money." He jumped out and rushed over to help her out of the truck. She'd never had a man open her car door for her before. The move did something to her insides, especially when he took her hand and held it as they walked into the pizzeria.

Could she afford to let someone like him close to her? She'd spent so much time protecting herself against outsiders that it was going to be hard to open herself up to him. Or to anyone, for that matter.

Still, there was that strange pull she felt towards him. As if they'd done this all before. She couldn't explain why she trusted him even though she'd only just met him.

As they were seated, she thought back to how wonderful it had felt showing off her abilities to the others the night before. How freeing it had felt. She'd been liberated and didn't want to go back to hiding in the shadows. But she knew she had to keep herself and her powers in check. Outside of the small circle of people last night, she doubted anyone would be so accepting of what she could do.

They had just been seated at a table near the back when Jess, Jacob, and Reed strolled in. When the family saw her and Colt, they headed back towards their table.

"Mind if we join you?" Jess asked, and Colt waved to the empty spots. Jess sat down while Jacob pulled another table towards theirs and sat down too.

"The others will be here soon," Jacob said. "We were just talking about you two," he added easily.

"Oh?" Colt asked.

"We've been texting each other all day about our next steps," Jacob continued.

"Steps?" Tara asked. "For?"

Jess leaned closer and lowered her voice. "To prepare for what's coming."

Tara tensed at Jess's words. "What makes you think something is coming?" she asked. Maybe it wasn't just her? What if Jess knew that she was the reason for the end of the world? What if she'd already told everyone else?

Jess's eyebrows shot up. "It's just a... feeling." She glanced over as Xtina, Mike, and Harper came in and made their way back towards them. The baby was set in her carrier on top of a child seat between the two parents. Shortly after, Ethan and Brea came in and joined them.

"So," Jess said after the entire group had ordered a few large pizzas. "Who is going to tell them?" She glanced around the table and was met with silence. Finally, she groaned. "Fine, I'll do it." She turned to Tara and Colt. "We think you two should be warned."

"About?" Colt asked.

Jess nudged Xtina, who quickly rolled her eyes. "That you're bound together."

"What?" Tara squeaked out. She hadn't meant to sound so alarmed.

Xtina held up her hands quickly. "Not... we're not saying

you're bound romantically or... anything like that." She looked at Jess for help.

"It goes beyond physical," Jess added. "It's..."

"Eternal," Brea broke in.

"Right," Jess said, pointing at Brea. "There's power." She motioned to everyone at the table. "Here and with everyone else you met last night."

"Power?" Colt asked with a frown.

"Some people have it," Xtina said, glancing around the table. "Others don't." She motioned to the rest of the people in the room.

"I don't have any power," Colt broke in with a shake of his head. "I mean, there's nothing special about me."

Tara had spent the last ten years ignoring the occasional illumination she saw surrounding certain people. She wasn't really sure what it meant or if it was even really there or just part of her imagination. But after meeting Jess and the rest of the gang yesterday, she knew it was real and more importantly, what it meant.

Tara turned towards Colt. "That's not true," she said to him, seeing the light surrounding him as clearly as she saw the glow around all the others in the room. "You have power just like the rest of them."

CHAPTER 8

Tara's words hit him hard for some reason. At first, he believed she was just trying to include him, but then he saw the truth in her eyes as she looked at him.

"How do you know?" he asked, his voice low. He didn't trust himself to maintain any hint of sanity. Sure, he'd accepted the other's abilities with little questioning. After all, in his life he'd seen a lot of amazing and crazy things happen. Besides, he was a pretty open-minded kind of guy. But him? Having any abilities? Nope. None. There was nothing special about him. Had never been. He was just… Colt.

"I can see it," Tara answered him. "In all of you." She motioned to the rest of the people at the table. "In them too," she said, nodding towards Reed and Harper with a smile. "Her light is almost as bright as your own," she said to Xtina.

Xtina's smile grew, and he watched as a tear of pride formed in her eyes. Mike reached over and took Xtina's hands in his.

"Reed's light is different than everyone else's," Tara said, looking at the little boy, who was happily chowing down on some crackers Jess had given him.

"Light?" Jess asked with a shake of her head. "As in aura? You can read auras?" she asked, sounding eager and impressed.

Tara looked slightly embarrassed for a moment. "I guess, if you can call it that. I mean, no one else has…" She glanced around the pizzeria. "Up until I met everyone last night, I didn't have any understanding of why I'd only seen it a few times. I thought I was just imagining it." She shook her head. "Now I'm sure it's something else." She looked around the table. "You all have it."

"What does it look like?" Jacob asked.

Tara shrugged slightly. "It's a faint light." She turned towards him, and he watched her run her eyes over him. Then she lifted her hand and hovered it just above his arm. "Floating just above the skin, like a glow. Most are a faint white, but Reed's…" She turned to the young boy. "His has a hint of… blue." Tara shook her head.

"I have it?" he asked, looking at his own hand.

"Yes." Tara smiled. "It's not distracting. Honestly, I don't even notice it until I focus." Her eyes narrowed again slightly, then she blinked and smiled as she shrugged. "See, now they're gone," she said just as their pizzas arrived.

"Okay," Jess said once everyone had started eating their pizza. "So that confirms it. Someone needs to take you two to the silo."

"Silo?" Colt asked, remembering a silo being mentioned in a few of the articles he'd read about the group and what had happened to them in the past few years. He knew all about military installations and missile silos. Hell, he'd spent more time than he'd like to admit sitting in such facilities, waiting for orders that could have very well destroyed and saved lives.

Jess nodded. "It's one of the most powerful places in

town. We're still not sure why, but it's where… everything went down."

"Okay," Tara said easily. "I'm game."

He glanced over at her, a little shocked that she'd be so willing.

"What? I'm here for answers." She set her drink down. "At this point, I'd do anything to get them."

After everyone was done with dinner, he thought about her words as they followed Jacob's truck out of town and back towards Xtina and Mike's place.

Since the silo had been locked up by the police after all the crazy events, Jacob was chosen to take them there. They stopped off at Mike's garage and loaded up with flashlights and other supplies they would need to explore the facility.

Tara was awfully quiet as they made their way through the trees and tall grass. Jacob chatted with them about the silo, giving them instructions on how to get to the main location safely. When they came to the open field, they turned to the left and stopped just outside of a small building.

"This is it," Jacob said, handing him a set of keys. "Here's the map to the main silo area." He handed Colt the map he'd been telling them about.

"You're not going to go in there with us?" Tara asked.

"No." Jacob glanced towards the doors. "It's perfectly safe. We've all agreed that this first time, it should be just the two of you." His eyes moved around, avoiding theirs.

"Thanks," Colt said, tucking the map into his jacket pocket. He turned and used the key Jacob had just given him to unlock the door.

"When you're done, make sure you lock it up tight again," Jacob called out as he headed back the way they'd come. They both watched the beam of his flashlight disappear into the trees.

"Something tells me he didn't want to go inside," Tara said, and Colt saw her shiver.

"He's probably been down here more times than he can count, considering everything that happened to them a couple years ago. He did get shot here, remember?" Colt reminded her.

"Right." She nodded.

"Shall we?" He held out his hand.

She looked down at it and took a deep breath. "Just so you know, it's not the dark I'll be afraid of down there. It's rats, spiders, and any other crawling things." She shivered visibly.

"The strongest woman on Earth is afraid of spiders." He chuckled and then added. "I've got your back. If I see anything, I'll smash it for you."

"Right." She rolled her eyes. "Tell me again, why we are doing this at night?" she asked as they stepped inside the door.

"Not sure," he admitted. "Want to come back tomorrow?"

She was silent for a moment, then she shook her head. "No, we're here now." She sighed. "Just… let's go see if we can find any answers."

"Yeah, about that. Do you know why they thought we'd find answers here?" he asked as they headed down the long narrow staircase. He went first, knocking a few cobwebs down for her.

When Tara remained silent for a while, he glanced over his shoulder at her.

"It's like a beacon," she said with a frown. "I can feel the pulse of power from here already."

He stopped at the base of the staircase and looked at her. They were almost eye to eye now, with her on the bottom step.

"You feel something?" he asked her.

She looked down at him. "Don't you?" she asked, watching his eyes.

He stopped, listened, opened himself to the possibilities for a moment, then shook his head. "No, nothing."

"You don't feel it yet," she said suddenly. "Come on, let's do some exploring." She took his hand and they walked down a narrow hallway. They passed through several smaller rooms and down another set of stairs, and then they finally stepped into the massive silo.

It was as if a wave of awareness washed over him. Goose bumps had his skin tingling.

"Now you feel it," she said, stepping into the room. The massive cover over the silo was shut tight. He used his flashlight and scanned the room; its beam barely traveled across the void to the other side.

He knew the hydraulics to lift the cover were probably far too old to work, yet he walked over and hit the lever regardless, flipping it several times with slight frustration.

"Need a hand?" she asked after a moment.

He glanced over at her and was about to turn her help down, but then he remembered who was standing next to him.

Smiling, he nodded to the darkness above them.

"You wouldn't want to pop up there and open the lid so we can have a little more light in here, would you?" he asked.

She was silent for a moment, and he thought she was going to deny him, but then she effortlessly lifted into the air. He shined his flashlight on her and held his breath when she disappeared into the darkness.

He heard the metal start to move before he saw the sliver of moonlight flood in from the opening.

When her shadow crossed in front of the moon as she lifted the cover all the way off, he snapped a photo of her on his cell phone. He didn't know why he'd taken it, other than he just wanted proof of how amazing she was.

To have such a power. His first thoughts were of how many people he could have saved overseas if he'd had half the strength she had. All the families that had been killed or destroyed in the war-torn areas he'd marched into. Even now, how many more were suffering that could be helped?

When she landed softly next to him, the moon's light brightening up the entire silo area, he asked her the question that burned in his mind.

"Why do you hide it?" he said, watching her reaction under the night sky.

Her eyebrows shot up for a moment, then she sat down on the concrete steps and patted the spot next to her.

He handed her a bottled water and watched her take a sip.

"I did tell you about Rob, right?" she said when she was done.

"Yeah, I mean, I get it. There's always going to be someone out there that will try and exploit someone like you." He frowned down at his hands. "But think of the good you could be doing." He looked back at her. "The lives that could be saved or changed for good." He shook his head. "It's got to outweigh the bad. Wouldn't it?"

Instead of answering, she glanced up at the moon that hung overhead.

"The few times I've tried to help others, it's always ended up badly," she said.

"How so?"

"Rob wasn't even the worse. I helped a young woman who I thought was being beat up in a random attack one night in Seattle. It turned out she'd just stolen an entire bag of drugs from her pimp. After I helped her escape, she turned around and sold those drugs to a bunch of high school students." She looked over at him. "The drugs had been laced and four students died. One is brain dead, and another will never function as an adult." She took another drink of the water. "What they don't show you in all the superhero movies is that it's hard to tell who is good and who is bad when you don't have the backstory. There isn't a guidebook for superheroing."

He glanced up at the stars. "So why do you think you have these abilities? Why you? Why the others?"

Instead of answering, she glanced up at the sky for a moment. "I have never told this to anyone else"—she glanced over at him— "but I'm pretty sure I'm from a different planet."

"Why exactly do you think that?" he asked. Maybe she was crazy. Maybe he was crazy.

She pointed to the sky. "The biggest hint is hovering about two hundred and thirty-nine thousand miles above us."

He glanced up and frowned. "The moon?" He balked. "You..." He shook his head. "Where you came from, you didn't have the moon?"

She shook her head. "There were two moons in our night sky, Selene and Tara." She smiled. "I was named after the smaller of the two."

He looked back at her, running his eyes over her face. Her long blonde hair almost glowed in the moonlight, and her piercing green eyes looked back at his as if she could see deeper into him than anyone else ever had.

"Okay." He took a deep breath. "Wow, let me try and process this."

She stood up and walked over to the middle of the room. Her shoulders slumped slightly.

He walked over and pulled her into his arms. "We'll figure

this out," he said just before he kissed her. The moment their lips met, he felt power surging through him. At first, he thought it was just from the intensity of his desire for her, but when his fingers and toes actually tingled, he opened his eyes. Then he took a step back.

"You… you're glowing," he gasped.

CHAPTER 9

Tara groaned inwardly and looked down at her brightly lit hands. "Does it freak you out?" she asked Colt, watching for his reaction.

To her surprise, he started laughing. At first, she thought maybe he was hysterical. Then he pulled her back into his arms and kissed her again, this time with more urgency.

"You are amazing. Everything you can do, it amazes me," he said between kisses. "My god, I don't want to stop kissing you."

"Then don't stop," she begged. "Please, Colt, I need..." She started to pull his jacket off his shoulders, but he stepped back.

"As much as I want to continue..." He glanced around. "This isn't exactly where I want to enjoy our first time together."

She smiled and nodded in agreement. "Okay." She took his hand and started walking towards the stairway, only to have him stop her.

"I think we'd better shut that. I'd hate for someone to accidently fall in." He motioned to the cover.

Sighing, she nodded in agreement and dropped his hand. Shutting the cover was a lot easier than opening it. Not that it had taken her any effort, but she had been so concerned about cobwebs or spiders that she'd gone very slow. With the added light of her skin glowing still, she got the cover back in place quickly.

Besides, what she hadn't told anyone was that she had to completely concentrate to use her abilities.

Once they were again shadowed in darkness, she took Colt's hand in hers and followed him back through the maze of rooms until they stepped outside again.

"My place or yours?" he asked with a chuckle.

"Yours," she answered easily, reaching up on her toes to kiss him. The light from her skin had dissipated finally. "Just as long as we can stop by my place so I can get a change of clothes for work tomorrow."

He smiled and took her hand in his and started walking back towards Xtina and Mike's place.

When they reached her place, he stood outside while she grabbed an overnight bag and threw in her clothes and her makeup kit. She stepped back out of her van and climbed into his truck when he opened the passenger door for her.

"It's going to take some time for me to get used to that," she said after he climbed in behind the wheel.

"What?" he asked, heading down the driveway.

"You, opening the door for me."

He glanced over at her. "You've never had someone open a car door for you?"

She shook her head. "No. I've seen it in movies, but..." She smiled. "I like it."

He smiled over at her. "Then I'll continue doing it." He was silent for a moment. "I didn't plan on this. Being drawn to you," he added.

She smiled over at him, enjoying the way he was squirming slightly. To her, that was a sign that whatever was between them was more than just sex. But since she'd known him less than a full day, she couldn't tell him that she too felt something… more. It was as if she had known him longer, as if they were connected, bound together, just like Jess had said.

When Colt parked at the hotel, she waited until he came around and opened her car door for her. Taking his hand, she followed him into the room. For a brief moment, she glanced around the standard hotel room. It was fairly new. She could still smell paint and new carpet, and everything looked fresh.

"Nice," she said as she set her bag down.

"Yeah, I was surprised myself. Most places I stay in are… well, not this nice," he said with a shrug.

"Want to talk about this?" she asked, seeing the look in his eyes.

Without saying anything, he moved over to the bed and sat down, then patted the spot next to him. She sat down next to him, taking his hand in hers.

"There's power here," she said, looking down at the pulse vibrating from their simple touch. "Power I've never felt or seen with anyone else." She glanced up into his eyes. "I know that I'm possibly just a job to you—"

"No," he interrupted. "You stopped being a job the moment I kissed you."

She smiled. "I'm the one who kissed you," she reminded him, causing him to chuckle.

"There's more here," he said, pulling her closer until his mouth was inches from hers. "I just don't want to screw this up."

"Then don't." She laid her mouth over his. The internal fire she'd felt the first time they'd kissed was back. Flames heated her soul as his hands pushed into her hair, holding her closer as his mouth slanted, taking the kiss deeper.

She couldn't remember a time that she'd wanted as much as she did now. What she was feeling for Colt was something she'd desired, dreamed about, all of her life.

"Please," she said, reaching to tug off his jacket. She needed to feel his skin against her own. To have his warmth, his hands, all over her.

He tossed off his jacket and helped her remove her own. He knelt before her and undid her tennis shoes, then toed off his own.

Instead of waiting for him to come back down to her, she stood up and, with her eyes locked on his, pulled his black T-shirt over his head. She let her eyes run over the toned muscles that filled his arms, his chest, and his narrow stomach. She smiled.

"Well?" he asked, getting her attention.

"Yum," she said with a chuckle. "Very impressive."

"My turn," he said, reaching for her shirt. She stood still while he helped her remove her top. She wasn't embarrassed at what she had or didn't have. She was proud of her B cups and her toned physique. She knew she was a few pounds too light, thanks to her inconsistent access to money and food, but at least she had enough muscle tone to avoid looking malnourished.

"Beautiful," he said, stepping back towards her. Her eyes closed when his hand came up to brush the back of his fingers against the curve of her breast. Then his mouth came back over hers.

"Colt," she moaned moments later when she felt her knees weaken. "Please."

"Since we're rushing everything else, in this, I'd like to take our time," he mumbled against her neck.

Her nails scraped over his shoulders as she tried to keep

herself centered and upright. She felt as if she was floating. No, scratch that. This feeling was much better than when she flew. This was as if every ounce of her being was tingling. Like she was anticipating the coming release and knowing that it would be the most exquisite feeling of her life.

She wanted to hold onto this feeling for as long as she could. She ran her hands down his sides, trailing her fingertips over every cord, every muscle, while enjoying the smoothness of his skin. When she came to a puckered scar, she glanced down and trailed a fingertip over the white mark.

"One of the reasons I'm no longer in the service," he said, glancing down at the scar with a slight frown. "It wasn't as bad as it looks."

She glanced up at him. "How long ago was that?"

"Three years ago." He cupped her face and met her eyes. "Then again, it's been a millennium since I first laid eyes on you."

This time when he kissed her, she felt his speed and urgency and instantly responded with her own. He backed her up until her knees hit the side of the bed. Then he was lifting her and laying her gently down on the bed. When he covered her with his own body, she wrapped her legs around his hips. She melted as his hands pushed the hem of her panties aside until he brushed his fingers across her skin. Everything else in the world faded into nothingness as light exploded behind her eyes.

"Yes, come for me, Tara," he begged her smoothly. "More, I need more." He moved down while he hoisted her hips up until he laid his mouth over her mound, lapping at the skin he'd just caused to vibrate.

She cried out, arched up, while her fingers tangled in his hair. This time when she exploded, she knew that her light was shining, that it burst from her uncontrollably.

"My god," he groaned as he moved up her body again. She felt him slide into her as her power built up once more. She hadn't believed she had more to give until she felt him inside her, consuming her, completing her. This. This was more than even she knew there could be.

Looking into Colt's eyes, she could see her destiny. She could see her future. She could see… everything.

Falling asleep in his arms some hours later after a shower and several more bouts of lovemaking, she began questioning just how they were going to make things work out. For the first time in her life, she believed she was surrounded by her people. Well, maybe not hers, but at least they got her. She didn't feel like she had to hide who she was. What she was.

She hadn't yet told them that she was from a different world, but she figured she'd get to that. After all, she had told Colt and he hadn't freaked. Maybe the others wouldn't either.

Tomorrow, she told herself. For now, she was going to enjoy the feeling of Colt surrounding her. The feeling of being cherished once more.

As she drifted off with a permanent smile on her lips, she began to dream. In this dream, she was back on the hill that held her castle home. The sun was shining overhead, the birds were singing, and she was happy. Turning in circles, she lifted her arms into the air and tried to fly. Only, she couldn't. Frowning, she looked down at her bare feet and frowned at the thick chains wrapped around her ankles.

"You can't show them what you are," a woman's voice said from behind her. "They wouldn't understand."

Tara turned to see a familiar blonde woman in a white flowing dress walking towards her, her arms stretched out as if waiting for a welcoming embrace.

"What am I?" she asked, looking down at her own

matching white dress. The light breeze caused the soft material to billow, making it appear as if she were a ship's sail, ready at any moment to take flight. But the chains wrapped around her ankles were keeping her grounded.

"You are the chosen." The woman smiled at her. "You are my second daughter. Destined to rule the stars one day."

Tara's eyes narrowed at the woman and for the first time, she realized why she looked so familiar.

"Mother?" she asked, shaking her head. "But you're dead."

Her mother smiled and shook her head. "Your father only believes what he was predestined to know."

"I… don't understand. Why did you leave me then?" she asked, tears coming to her eyes.

"Because, my daughter, it was not my place." She tilted her head and looked at her. "You must let your power continue to grow. You must learn to love and trust for you to shine. It is your destiny. Your purpose."

"Purpose?" she asked, glancing around. "I don't understand?"

"There are some that would take your power from you. Now that it has grown, they will come for you and your sister as well," her mother said with a slight frown.

"My… I have a sister?" Tara asked, shaking her head.

Her mother smiled slightly. "Selene. One day, you two are destined to meet. Soon. Your power combined might just be enough."

"Enough?" She shook her head. "I don't…" But then the darkness that had consumed everything that she'd loved on her sixteenth birthday started to grow behind her mother. She screamed and reached out, begging for her mother to run. Instead, her mother's smile grew.

"Soon, I will find you. Look out for me at the last full moon," she said. Then her figure faded with a flash of white light, just before the darkness would have consumed her.

"No!" Tara called out, jolting herself awake from the dream.

"Easy." Colt's deep voice soothed her. "I'm right here."

"No." She shook him off, trying to free herself from his hold. "I have to go to her."

"Who?" Colt asked, after turning on a light by the bed. His eyes searched hers, and she could see the worry in them.

"My mother," she answered, rolling out of bed to pull on her clothes.

"Hey." Colt took her arm. "It's okay, it was just a dream. We can start looking in the morning."

"No." Tara sat down on the bed and let him wrap his arms around her. "Something's coming. I can feel it." She did. From the moment she woke up, she could feel the darkness hunting her. Closing her eyes, she leaned back against Colt's chest. He was right. There was nothing she could do now, in the middle of the night.

But there was something hunting her and her sister… She had a sister. She would have to think about that in the morning. Until then, all she could do was hold onto the man she was connected to.

The man she knew that, soon enough, she would grow to love. This too, was her destiny. Just as her mother had said.

CHAPTER 10

Whatever Tara's nightmare had been about, Colt knew that she hadn't gotten much more sleep. When her alarm went off, he woke with her, and they both dressed in silence.

"You don't have to come in with me," she said as he slipped on his shoes and jacket.

He could hear the rain and thunder outside and grabbed his umbrella. The forecast called for rain all week.

"I don't have to, but I'm hoping for a cup of joe and something sugary to jolt me awake and fill my empty stomach." He pulled her into his arms, enjoying her softness against his chest. He kissed her and felt her relax slightly. "Besides, I figured the coffee shop is as good a place to work as any. That is, if you want me to find your mother?"

She glanced up at him. "You…" He watched tears form in her eyes. "Thank you," she said softly.

When they stepped into the coffee shop, Jess was already there, taking the chairs off the tables.

"Here." He walked over and started grabbing chairs. "Let me help."

Jess smiled at him. "Thanks. I suppose you deserve a hot scone for helping."

He smiled. "I wouldn't turn one away." He finished setting the last chair down.

"I'll grab you one while Tara makes you both some coffee. Something tells me the two of you could use the boost," she added with a wink.

"Before we open," Tara said to Jess as she got to work making them their drinks, "I want to tell you what happened."

"Later," Jess said with a wave of her hand. "Everyone's coming over after we close. If you can hold out that long?" she asked, setting two blueberry scones on plates.

"I can." Tara nodded. "I suppose it would be better to tell everyone at the same time."

"Always is," Jess said and set a plate in front of him.

"If you don't mind, I was going to set up shop here today?" he asked Jess.

"I don't mind." Jess leaned closer and lowered her voice so that Tara didn't hear. "She looks exhausted. Happy, but..." Jess's eyes narrowed. "Worried."

He nodded. "Bad dreams," he whispered.

"I can still hear you," Tara said dryly.

"We're just worried about you." Jess laid a hand on Tara's arm. "But, to compensate for the lack of sleep, you'd better make yours a double shot." She motioned to the espresso machine.

When Tara set his coffee in front of him, he motioned to the chair. "Got just a moment? I'll need some information from you."

She sat down across from him and nibbled on her scone.

"What's your mother's name?" He opened his laptop and waited for it to boot up.

She sighed and lowered her voice as she glanced over at

Jess, who was busy counting the money and opening the register.

"Something tells me that you won't find her. Seeing as I'm pretty sure I came from another planet and all," she said softly.

"It won't hurt at least trying." He took her hand in his. "It's worth a shot."

She remained silent for a moment, and he could tell she was thinking. Then she nodded quickly.

"Rhea," she answered finally. "Her name was Rhea."

His eyebrows shot up. "Rhea?"

"Yes." She frowned at his look.

"Tara, that's..." He shook his head. "My client's name is Rhea Cybele. Could this be your mother?"

She looked surprised for a moment then leaned back in the chair.

"I don't know her maiden name. For all I know, her name was Rhea Dawson. My father told me that she had died shortly after my birth. Two years later he married my step-mother Robin. I didn't even know Robin wasn't my real mother until I was thirteen when I found a picture of my father and... my real mother." She shook her head, and he could see sadness in her eyes. "It was as if I'd found a part of myself. As if I hadn't known something was missing until then." She glanced over at the clock. He knew that there was less than five minutes before they opened their doors to customers. He could see a few cars parking in the lot already.

"She mentioned that I have a sister," Tara said, looking at him. "Selene."

His eyebrows shot up. "Dawson or Cybele?" He typed the name in his file next to her mother's name.

"I don't know." She shook her head. "I..." She glanced over at Jess and lowered her voice again. "I don't think she was from the same place I was," she added, seeing that Jess was watching them. "I'd better get to work."

"Last question. What's your father's name?" he asked.

"Jason." She stood up. "If your client is my mother, will you contact her?"

"Not until I'm sure." He took her hand again. "I want to ensure that you're safe before I make any moves."

She smiled slightly and nodded. "Thanks." She leaned down and placed a soft kiss on his lips, then turned and opened the front door and got to work.

For the next hour, he searched for both Rhea and Tara's sister Selene, using both the last names Dawson and Cybele. Then he tried looking for her father Jason. It didn't help that there were more than a hundred Jason Dawsons in California alone. It was a pretty common name. Cybele, on the other hand, was fairly unique. Still, when the first morning rush of customers had died down, he hadn't come up with any answers.

"Problems?" Jess asked as she set a large brownie down in front of him.

"Not anymore." He smiled and took a bite of the treat. "If I keep eating like this, I may have to hit the gym."

Jess sat down across from him. "You're welcome to use Mike's weights in the garage. Jacob, Ethan, and Mike meet three times a week and try to outlift each other." She rolled her eyes as she smiled.

"Sounds fun." He glanced towards Tara, who was washing mugs in the sink near the back. "How's she doing today?"

"Good. She's by far one of my best workers," Jess admitted. "So, the two of you..." Jess leaned on the table and watched his expression.

"Yeah, appears so," he said, glancing back over at Tara. "I mean, there definitely is something there."

"Good. I tried to fight it with Jacob." She frowned slightly.

"Afraid of what I'd seen, afraid of the possibilities. But if I've learned one thing over the past few years, it's that fate can be changed." She smiled. "Changed with the power of love and friendship."

He was surprised at Jess's words, and they ran over in his mind long after she went back to work with the second wave of customers.

Around lunchtime, he ran across the street and grabbed the three of them take-out orders, then sat in the back room with Tara and ate a burger while she was on break.

They kept the conversation light, talking about his past, his family, his time in the military. It was nice being able to flirt and talk to someone as easily as he could with her. He didn't have to work hard at it since he felt very natural being around her. More so than he'd felt for anyone else before.

When the coffee shop closed at two, Jess turned off the open sign.

"Want to help clean up before the others get here?" she asked him.

"Sure." He shut down his laptop and helped them flip most of the chairs up on the tables again and then swept the floors while Tara and Jess cleaned up behind the counter.

"Is this place always this busy?" he asked Jess as he worked.

"Yes," she answered with a smile. "Thankfully."

"You never did say if you own the business?" he asked.

"Technically, my mother does, but since she's trapped on the moon..." She shrugged and continued counting out the dollar bills.

"Right." He shook his head. "I'm still having a hard time wrapping my mind around that bit of news."

Jess laughed. "I guess you would have had to have been there to believe it." She sighed and zipped the bank bag and then tucked it in her bag. "There's my man now." She smiled as she looked at the front door.

He finished sweeping as Jacob walked in holding Reed.

"Guess who learned a new word today?" Jacob said, handing Reed over to Jess.

"Shit!" the boy shouted happily.

He couldn't help it, a chuckle escaped his lips. Jess looked over at him, then turned back to her husband and asked in a sweet voice, "And where did our son learn this new word?"

Jacob shook his head. "Not from me." He turned and pointed to Xtina as she walked in the door.

"Sorry," Xtina said apologetically. "It just… slipped out."

Jess chuckled. "Wait until my son teaches it to your daughter." She kissed her son several times until the boy forgot all about shouting the new word he'd learned and giggled instead.

Less than ten minutes later, everyone from the other night was packed in the coffee shop, waiting for Tara to talk.

He squeezed Tara's hand under the table to encourage her when she remained silent for a moment.

"My mother visited me last night in my sleep," she began. "She claims something is coming." Her eyes ran over everyone else. "Like you hinted at."

"Did she let you know what it was?" Jess asked, not missing a beat.

He was a little shocked that no one around the table seemed to be put off that Tara's mother had visited her in a dream. Instead, everyone started asking questions as if it were the most natural thing.

He listened as Tara filled everyone in on what had transpired. She hesitated for a moment before letting everyone in on the fact that she was from another world. To his surprise, Joleen chimed in.

"Oh, I'm from another world too," she said with a smile. "I wonder if it's the same one?"

Tara's eyes grew wide. "You are?"

Joleen nodded easily. "The short version is that parallel universes exist. In my world, my mother is a scientist and found a way for me to escape it before my half-brother, Thanatos, destroyed it and took over."

Everyone was silent for a moment. "Okay," Tara said finally. "Did you have a moon?" she asked, and for the first time everyone around the table looked slightly shocked.

"Yes," Joleen answered.

"One?" Tara asked. Joleen nodded, and Tara sank back. "Then we're not from the same place."

"Didn't you have a moon?" Xtina asked.

"We had two of them. Selene and Tara. Last night my mother informed me that I have an older sister named Selene. Which led me to believe that my sister was thrust into this world like I was on my sixteenth birthday."

"I've been looking for her all day," he added in. "Without any luck." His eyes went to Tara's.

He could see the sadness and felt as much frustration as she did in not finding anything. But since he didn't know how much older she was than Tara, or even a last name, he'd had little to go on.

"We can lend you a hand," Mike suggested.

Colt nodded. "I'll take any help you want to give."

"It can't be Thanatos," Joleen said. "I dealt with him," she added with a smile.

"All I know is that it's a darkness and, from what I can tell, it consumed my world," Tara said.

"Sounds like Thanatos," Ethan said dryly.

"Whatever or whomever we have to deal with, did your mother say when they were coming?" Xtina asked.

Tara glanced down at her fingers, and Colt reached over to take her hand in his.

"At the full moon," she answered, almost whispering. "I don't know…"

"The Harvest Moon," several people said in unison. When both he and Tara looked at them, Jess shrugged.

"We've been doing this a while," she said with a sigh. She pulled out her phone. "Two weeks," she said after a moment and relaxed back.

"Okay, so we have some time to figure things out." Xtina also relaxed back in her chair.

He frowned, looking around the table. Everyone appeared relieved by this news. Had they really gone through everything he'd read and heard about in the past two years? Normal people didn't sit around and talk about fighting off gods as casually as they were.

Still, he sat back and listened as everyone started planning just how they were going to protect the planet from whatever darkness was coming. While he and Tara listened, he held her hand under the table and knew that he was willing to stick by her side. No matter what they were about to face.

CHAPTER 11

Tara closed her eyes and listened to Colt's heartbeat against her ear. The rhythm had settled from its fast pace moments earlier. She could get very used to spending her nights wrapped around him.

They'd spent their evening taking another hike out to the silo, only this time with Jess and Jacob, since Xtina agreed to watch Reed.

Jess had suggested the trip and hoped to discover something they could use to help them in the fight.

Here was another thing she could get used to in life. Having people believe her and trust her. Not to mention the lack of judgment and no threats of exposing her.

It helped that each of the group had their own secrets they wanted to hide from the world.

While they had hiked out to the silo, Jess had questioned her about everything she could remember about the day of her birthday. If she'd seen a creature in the darkness, heard anything, felt anything.

Since she had no comparison to what they'd experienced with Thanatos, she was at a complete loss. In all her memories, the only time she'd felt scared was when she'd seen the moon in the night sky for the very first time. Selene was only half the size of the moon and Tara a quarter of the size of Selene.

Even now, any time she looked up at the full moon, she got chills.

"Are you okay?" Colt asked, his hand running over her bare shoulder.

"Yes." She smiled, realizing she'd shivered at her own thoughts. "Just… remembering when I came here."

"Losing your entire world must have been hard," he said, his arms tightening around her waist.

"Do you think…" She dropped off, biting her lip, not willing to ask what she'd been thinking since hearing Joleen's story.

"Hmm?" he asked, shifting her until she looked down at him. The dim light from the bathroom shadowed his features, making him look even more attractive and mysterious. "What?"

"Do you think there's a chance my dad and stepmother are still alive? That my world wasn't destroyed like Joleen's?" she asked.

Colt was silent for a moment, then reached over and flipped on the lamp by the bed and looked at her.

"If there is a slight possibility, would you want to go back?" he asked, his eyes searching hers.

"I… don't know. I spent sixteen years there." She saw something close to fear cross his features as his arms tightened around her. "But… I was a child. So much has probably changed. I've changed." She felt him relax. "I would like to see my father and stepmother. To know that they are safe." She rested her head against his chest again.

"Joleen and Mason said they returned to her home planet or universe or whatever," he said with a shrug.

"It all seems so… overwhelming. Doesn't it?" she said after a moment. His chuckle had her glancing up at him. "What?"

"Honey, the moment I saw you lift a piano like it weighed nothing, I stopped being surprised by anything." He kissed the top of her head. "Now, let's get some sleep. Your shift starts too early for my liking." He turned off the light and scooted them back down to lay on the bed.

"You don't have to go with me," she suggested.

"I like it. Besides, it's a good place for me to work. Beats sitting in here all by myself," he mumbled.

"Colt?" she said after a moment.

"Hmm?"

"Thank you for being here with me. For not… freaking out," she said, feeling foolish.

She felt his chest rumble as he laughed. "Oh, I'm freaking out, just… hiding it very well."

"Well, thanks for hiding it then." She leaned up and kissed his stubbly chin.

She didn't want to admit it, but she was having a difficult time shutting down. She was afraid that if she fell asleep, once again her mother would deliver bad news.

For a few moments, she listened to Colt's breathing and his heartbeat as he drifted into deep slumber. When she knew he was fast asleep, she slipped out of the bed, pulled on Colt's T-shirt, and tiptoed into the bathroom, taking her phone with her.

Sitting on the edge of the bathtub, she pulled up the browser and did a few searches for her sister. When she came up empty-handed, she shut her phone down and glanced into the mirror.

A sister. What would she look like? Obviously, Selene was a half-sister, since her father would have told her if he'd had another daughter. Wouldn't he? Then again, they hadn't told her that Robin was her stepmother until she'd been in her teens. Maybe they had kept it a secret, to protect her?

Whatever the reason, she doubted that her father and stepmother would have kept a sister from her.

She was so deep in her thoughts that, at first, the darkness that surrounded her hadn't registered. Then she heard the low chuckle.

"What's wrong little goddess?" The voice was almost a hiss.

With the knowledge that she was surrounded, also came the awareness that she was no longer sitting in the hotel bathroom. Instead, she stood at the base of the silo, still wearing only Colt's T-shirt.

The heavy door that she'd opened before now sat wide, letting the moonlight stream into the large space.

For a moment, she thought she'd imagined the voice. Maybe she was still tucked warmly against Colt and dreaming?

"No, daughter, you are not dreaming." The hiss was back.

She did a full circle, scanning the dark shadows, looking for who was talking.

"Who are you?" she called out, her voice echoing in the space. She didn't feel safe, so she lifted up off the ground to float halfway between the lid and the floor. Here, she could at least look down at her enemy.

"I'm hurt," the voice said with sarcasm, much closer to her than before, "that you don't remember me."

When the figure stepped out of the darkness, she realized her mistake. The creature's head brushed the top of the silo. It's green piercing eyes were narrow slits that glowed in the darkness. She couldn't see the rest of the man, but other than the snake-like eyes, he appeared normal. Giant, but normal.

She hadn't thought herself a small person, at five foot ten

inches. But hovering just in front of the man's face, she figured she was only as long as his nose.

She was seriously outgunned. Thoughts of trying to make a run for it played in her head quickly, until the man laughed.

"You can try to run," he said with a smile. "Your mother has hidden you from me for years." He shook his head. "Now that I've found you, it's only a matter of time before I come for you."

She frowned at his words. If he was going to come for her, that meant… He wasn't really here now?

She tried to sense herself. Her mother had appeared to her in a dream. Maybe this man, whoever he was, could project into her mind as well and make her believe she was back in the silo.

"Who are you?" she said again, this time a little firmer.

"I am Typhon." The man's words echoed loudly, causing her ears to ring and the entire silo to shake. His eyes narrowed as he leaned closer to her, a smile causing his white teeth to glimmer in the moonlight. "Your father, and I am here for what I am due."

"Tara!" Colt shook her as he screamed her name several more times.

It took her a few seconds to break out of the trance. When she finally did, she wrapped her arms around Colt and held onto him while she wept.

The following day, she once more sat around a table and explained what had happened to her. This time, everyone was gathered back at Xtina's place.

Since the rain had not let up in two days, they were gathered in the large dining area. Someone had grabbed burgers and fries from the local burger joint, and Joe had brought the beer and wine.

As she told them what had happened, she realized that in the few days she'd known everyone, not only had she and

Colt grown close, but for the first time in her life, she trusted. Everyone sitting around the table knew what it was like to be different. To be… something more.

No matter whether it was a seer, a witch, an oracle, or a demi-god, at least they had one thing in common. They all believed in something bigger.

"Okay, who the frack is Typhon?" Jess asked, glancing over at her son, who was sitting in his father's lap.

"Typhon…" Mason said, pulling out his laptop. "Serpentine giant, a god, most deadly creature in Greek mythology… great." He glanced around the table and shook his head, then returned to his computer. "And father of all monsters."

Tara felt a shiver down her spine. "He called me his daughter."

Colt reached over and took her hand. "You're not a monster."

"None of us are," Joleen said.

"I did some research on who I think your mother is," Mason added. "Would you like…" He started to ask.

"Tell me," Tara said, feeling her entire body tense. "I need to know." Colt squeezed her hand lightly.

"I'm here," he said softly.

Mason nodded. "Rhea, goddess of nature. Daughter of the Earth goddess Gaia and the sky god Uranus. Known as the mother of gods."

"Okay, so the mother of gods and the father of monsters…" Jess said, looking over at her.

"This is just mythology," Mason added in.

"Myths have served us well so far," Xtina said.

"What of my father?" she asked softly, feeling her heart skip in her chest. "The man who raised me?"

"Parents don't have to be biological," Joleen said. "My mother was…" She closed her eyes and took a deep breath. "She did what she had to do. She found a young couple who would love me as much as she did. She ensured my survival and that I was raised with love. Maybe that's what your mother did to protect you?"

She had never thought about it like that. Since the moment she'd found out that Robin was her stepmother and that her mother had died, she'd only been thinking of herself and her loss.

But since the other night, she'd been angry at her mother for leaving her. For deceiving her and her father all those years.

Could it be true? Was… the man she'd seen last night her real father?

"You said serpentine?" she asked, remembering the man's voice. How he'd almost hissed his words. Instantly she felt a shiver race through her.

"Yeah." Mason clicked on his computer. "There's a sketch." He turned the computer, showing a black-and-white line drawing of a giant with serpent legs, more snakes for hands and his head in the clouds.

"The… man I saw was human. Tall, but human," she answered. "He did, however, hiss slightly when he spoke.

"Okay, so let's assume we're working with the one and only father of monsters. What can we expect?" Jess asked Mason.

"He apparently has wings that are so big that they'll blot out the sun. He can shoot fire from his eyes. Oh, and he not only commands snakes, but dragons." Mason glanced up through his reading glasses. "So there's that. Even the Olympians were afraid of him."

"Someone had to defeat him though, right?" Xtina asked. "I mean, the bad guy always gets his butt kicked. Right?"

Mason read for a moment, then nodded. "He tried to overthrow Zeus and got his ass sent to Tartarus." Mason looked at Tara. "Hell, basically." He glanced back down at the computer screen. "Or Mount Etna. There are mixed stories."

It was all so much to take in. Feeling slightly overwhelmed, she pushed her half-eaten burger away and took a sip of her beer.

"What else can you tell us?" Xtina asked. "Anything we can use against him?"

When everyone sitting around the table looked at her, she felt even more overwhelmed. Her new friends were relying on her. The entire world was relying on her. And she had nothing. No hints into how to win the fight, how to save the world, or even herself.

As far as she knew, Typhon was coming. Her mother was coming.

The only thing she did know was that she was in the right place, surrounded by the right people to fight the darkness.

The most important part had been that she'd found Colt. As far as she could tell, he was willing to stick by her side through it all.

CHAPTER 12

With less than two weeks to go until the Harvest Moon, the group of friends decided to meet each night. Each day after Tara's shift, she and Colt spent a few hours alone together before meeting the rest of the gang.

Most nights their meetings were at Xtina and Mike's place. Other times they gathered at either the diner or the pizza place in town.

It was funny. When it was just the two of them, they pretended as if the world wasn't about to end. As if they were a normal couple, spending their time enjoying one another.

They went on hikes, watched movies, even went shopping. Normal things that normal couples did.

He knew that they were just biding their time until her parents showed up. Until the darkness came and took her away. Or the planet was destroyed. Neither outcome was his ideal choice.

So he tried to spend as much enjoyable time with Tara as he could.

Today's adventure had been clothes shopping. Since he needed a few more basics. Mainly, a warmer jacket, since the weather had taken a turn after all the rain they'd gotten. He'd never spent a fall in the south, but everyone was assuring him that the chill in the night air wasn't normal.

He wondered if it had anything to do with what was coming but didn't want to voice his concerns. The group had enough on their minds, trying to figure out a defense.

He'd convinced Tara to move into the hotel room with him temporarily. There was enough space for the two of them without him bumping his head, like in her van, so she'd agreed. He was thankful for it. He'd had a few long-term relationships in his past, but thus far hadn't lived with anyone. At least not beyond a few single night sleepovers.

Each night, he could tell she was growing more restless. She didn't sleep more than a few hours and when she was asleep, he often had to wake her up from her nightmares.

She claimed that her mother or her father visited her on a regular basis, and each evening she would go over what had transpired in her dreams.

He had to admit, just hearing what her father was like every evening scared him. If everything she was saying was true, the man was not only a giant, but pure evil.

"We're always in the silo," she told the group that evening.

Once again, with the rain outside, everyone was gathered in Xtina and Mike's place, this time in the living room. A fire was going, and everyone sipped hot tea or hot chocolate and nibbled on the chocolate chip cookies Jess had brought along.

"The place holds power," Xtina said.

"It's where we banished Thanatos," Mike added.

"It goes beyond that," Liz said. He had noticed that Liz didn't speak very often, but when she did, the entire group hung on every word she said. "There is power in the soil, in the deepness of it. Before the silo, there had been a cave that was just as powerful."

"The cave," Brea said with a shiver. Ethan reached over and took her hand in his. "I... I've been there. Before." She shook her head. "Before I could control my powers."

"You still can't some of the time," Jess added with a smile.

"True, but back then they were going really crazy. There's the other entrance to the silo. The one through the cave," Brea said.

"So the place holds power," Jess said with a shrug.

"We all hold power," Joleen added. "Maybe all of us working together can send Typhon back where he belongs."

"Have you seen anything?" Mike asked Jess.

"No, there's something blocking..." She stopped, gasped, then jumped up. "I need wine." She disappeared into the kitchen.

Colt heard Jess rummaging around in the kitchen.

"Joe, you'd better go help..." Xtina started only to have the man quickly disappear. Quickly being the key word. One second the man was there, the next he wasn't.

Then he was back, only this time he walked in slowly, holding a tray of glasses. Jess was behind him, carrying a bottle of wine.

"Sorry, there's only one bottle..." Jess started to say, but then Joe disappeared again and less than a minute later was back with two more bottles.

"I'll help pour," Mike said as he opened one of the bottles. "We keep the glasses around," Mike started, "for when we need a look at what's coming."

"Okay," Tara frowned down at the glass she'd been handed.

"They're crystal," Xtina explained. "They'll harness the energy, focus it." She scooted in and held her glass up.

As everyone did the same, they all looked towards Jess and waited.

Jess chuckled. "Okay, I've been saving this one..." She

held up her glass, took a deep breath, and then said, "Here's to those who wish us well; all the rest can go to hell." Jess smiled and then they all moved their glasses together.

The moment the sound of crystal clinking together reached his ears, everything went dark. He thought he heard someone scream, but when he looked about, he was alone in a very large room made of marble.

Glancing around, one of the first things he realized was how warm it was. The second was that he was wearing a toga.

Where the hell was he? He desperately looked around again for more clues.

The furniture, what furniture there was in the massive room, was odd looking, old-fashioned, and it looked extremely uncomfortable.

He turned when he heard footsteps rushing towards him.

He relaxed when he saw Tara rush into the room dressed in a long flowing gown. It was almost the same style as his toga, but it was a pale rose color. Her blonde hair was far longer and pulled up in an intricate bun. Gold earrings swung from her ears as she rushed towards him. Her matching rings and bracelets gleamed in the bright daylight.

"There you are," she said, taking his hands. "You must go now before my husband finds you."

"Tara?" he asked, shaking his head. "What... Where are we?"

Tara frowned up at him. "Cyrus, we don't have time for games." She tugged on his arm. "You must go before Magnus returns. If he finds you here..."

He stopped Tara from pulling him towards the door. "Tara?" He shook his head. She turned and when she looked into his eyes, he realized that she wasn't his Tara. Yes, this was the woman he knew, but there, deep in her eyes there was something... missing.

Taking a step back, he shook his head. "This isn't right." He felt everything fade to black again.

This time when he opened his eyes, he stood in a diner as loud oldies music played. He vaguely remembered the song as one that his grandmother had always enjoyed on the radio station she listened to when she drove.

He glanced down at his clothes and frowned at the sneakers, the worn rolled-up jeans, and the button-up shirt he was wearing.

"There you are, Bobby," someone said from behind him.

Turning, he watched Tara stand up from a booth and head towards him. This time she was dressed in a medium length cream skirt that flared out around her legs. She wore black-and-white dress shoes and a soft-pink button-up top. Her long blonde hair was cut shorter, in a curly hairdo that framed her face.

"I thought you'd never get here," she said, taking his hand. "Jenny was just telling me about the dance." She tugged him towards the booth she'd just come from.

"Tara?" he said, taking her hands and stopping her again. "What's going on?"

She looked up into his eyes and smiled. "Who's Tara, silly?" She giggled and playfully slapped his shoulder.

He took a step back and dropped her hand just as everything went dark once more.

Each time he visited a new place and time, it was the same. He was there, then Tara would come, calling for him with a different name, dressed in strange clothes, in a variety of cultures.

He lost count of how many separate places they had been. How many lives flashed before his eyes?

When it all finally came to a halt, he was standing in the base of the silo, watching Tara, his Tara, kiss him for the first time, only days ago.

"We've been circling one another for centuries," a voice said directly beside him.

He glanced over, and Tara took his hand in hers. "It's no wonder we felt an instant draw to one another." She smiled over at him.

"Did you know?" he asked, feeling slightly off balance.

"Not until now. You?" she asked.

He turned to her and once again they were surrounded by darkness, as if pulled into a new place. One where there was only the two of them.

"No," he answered and bent his head down to kiss her. "But this feels…"

"Right," she replied with a sigh.

He nodded. "Reincarnation?" he asked.

"Whatever it is"—she looked up into his eyes— "the only steady factor in my life has been you."

CHAPTER 13

*S*itting around Xtina and Mike's living room and listening to everyone fill each other in on what they had experienced during their… moment was one of the strangest things Tara had ever done.

She and Colt had been the last to wake from the trance. Seeing everyone stand over them when she woke, she hadn't known everyone else had experienced anything until they had all started talking.

It appeared that most of them had witnessed a coming event in the silo. Once again, they were all gathered around in a circle. Only this time, they weren't fighting Thanatos. This time they were all pitted against one another.

"I don't know what caused the fight," Jess said, "but I was kicking some serious butt." She turned to her husband. "Your butt," she added with a smirk.

"Right." Jacob laughed. "The way I saw things, I had you right where I wanted you." He wiggled his eyebrows.

"But you were fighting, right?" Mike asked.

"Sure, but…" Jess started.

"There is no way that would ever happen," they both said together.

"Okay, so what? What we just saw was a lie?" Xtina asked. "Because there are times Mike may piss me off, but I can't ever imagine bashing him over the head like…" She visibly shivered.

"Yeah, I was hoping that wasn't going to really happen," Mike added, rubbing his head. "I guess I need to hit the flower shop when I'm in town next."

"Let's assume that what we all just witnessed was a lie," Jess said. "Did anyone see anything different than all of us in the silo fighting one another?"

"Yes," Colt said, taking her hand.

She sat there while he explained what he'd seen and remained silent. She had witnessed everything he had, but there were some differences.

While he'd said that he was in the scenes, she'd watched from far away, almost as if she had been watching the scenes unfold on a television.

When Colt was done telling his tale, everyone watched them.

"So, what, reincarnation?" Xtina asked.

"No," she said softly, getting everyone's attention.

"How do you know?" Colt asked her.

"Because, in each life, we were tied to one another," she said simply.

"Fated," Jess said softly. Then she visibly shivered and stood up quickly. "I'm done for the night," she said with a yawn. "You have the day off tomorrow." She turned to Tara. "I still have to be in to work early, so I'm calling it a night." She bent down and picked up her son, who had been playing with a toy truck.

Colt held her hand as they left with everyone else. They walked back out to his truck.

When they got to the hotel, he helped her out of the truck and pulled her into his arms. "You're quiet," he said, running his eyes over her face.

"I…" She shook her head. "How about a walk?" she asked, motioning towards the small park near the hotel.

"Sure." Colt took her hand and headed off across the parking lot. "At least the rain has stopped."

"It's still cold, but living in the Northwest, I suppose you are used to it," she said, pulling her jacket closer around her.

"Somehow it's colder here." He shook his head. "I suppose because there's more moisture in the air." He sighed and stopped by the swing set. "Want to tell me what is on your mind?" he said, motioning for her to sit down.

When she did, he started pushing the swing lightly, sending her back and forth.

She took a deep breath, enjoying the swaying.

"I saw my death," she blurted out.

Colt grabbed the chain and stopped the swing, then stepped in front of her. The light from the parking lot washed over them, and she could see he had a serious look his face.

"You did?" he asked.

"Not… I mean, all of my deaths. In…" She waved her hand. "In our past lives or whatever it was we saw."

"Oh," he said softly. "That must have been hard." He frowned. "All of them?" She nodded. He pulled her up and into his arms. "I'm sorry."

"You didn't see yours?" she asked, somehow already knowing the answer.

"No, just… flashes of moments."

She nodded her head. "Good." She sighed.

"Why?" He pulled back and looked down at her.

She took a deep breath, took a step back, and looked him

in the eyes. "Because each one of my deaths, in one way or another, was because of you."

He was silent for a moment. "What the hell?" He turned away from her and ran his hands through his hair. "What am I supposed to do with that knowledge?" he asked. She understood he wasn't asking her, not really. He paced for a moment, then he turned back to her, and she could see his worry.

Walking back over to him, she wrapped her arms around him. "You never hurt me yourself. I know you'd never do that." She pulled him down to place her lips over his. "Each time, it broke your heart that I was gone."

He rested his forehead on hers. "No, I'd never hurt you," he agreed. "Now we know, at least, why it feels like we've known each other forever." He looked into her eyes. "It's been several lifetimes."

She smiled. "That doesn't diminish how much I want you," she said, taking his hand. "For now, let's enjoy one another."

He nodded and started walking her back to their hotel room. The moment the door shut behind them, his mouth covered hers. The kiss was familiar yet felt new with the added passion. Each time they'd been together before now, he'd been gentle, passionate, and had taken it slow. Now, however, there was a renewed urgency. As if they both knew they had less than a week left together.

There was something building in both of them, and she was desperate to get her hands on him. All of him.

She pushed his jacket off his shoulders and then yanked his T-shirt over his head. Then she leaned down to run her teeth over his shoulder.

"Tara," Colt growled out, but she reached for the buckle on his jeans.

"You feel it too," she said, trailing her mouth down his

chest until she took his flat nipple into her mouth and sucked until he groaned.

Then he switched their positions, pushing her jacket and shirt off her until she was bare for him. He backed her up against the door as his mouth trailed the same pathway on her as she had on him.

She arched and moaned his name as he nudged her bra aside to uncover one of her erect nipples, taking it into his mouth and sucking. Her fingernails dug into his hair as he trailed his mouth over her skin, causing goose bumps to rise everywhere.

"Colt," she cried out when his hands moved down her back, her sides, and cupped her rear. He hoisted her up until she wrapped her legs around him and carted her towards the bed.

They fell on the mattress in a heap. His mouth covered hers again as they raced to remove the rest of their clothing. They were both a little breathless when the last of the barriers were removed.

"I want to watch you come for me," he growled next to her inner thigh as his breath washed over her. "I want to taste you," he said, covering her, using his tongue to bring her to the edge.

"Please." She closed her eyes, feeling the tears build up, fearing that what they had wouldn't last. She felt, somehow, that this time would be the last. Keeping her eyes closed tightly, she shook her head and held onto that moment. She needed it. Needed him. As much as he needed her.

"Come for me," Colt begged. "Let go," he said against her skin.

When the lights exploded behind her eyes and she felt everything that had built up inside her release, she cried out.

"Shh, I'm here," Colt said softly next to her ear.

"Please stay," she said with a sigh.

"I'm not going anywhere," he said, slowly slipping into her.

She wrapped herself around him, trying to hold onto him. Willing the moment to last many more lifetimes, even as she knew it wouldn't.

For the first time in days, she fell asleep easily in his arms afterwards. Thankfully, she had a few hours of peaceful slumber before the dreams took her.

Tonight, thankfully, it was her mother's turn to appear to her.

"I'm almost there my sweet," she said in a soothing voice. This time they were in a field. The sky was filled with the bright colors of a sunset. She could just make out the stars in the distant darkening sky. She stood in a white billowing dress, much like her mother wore herself. Her long blonde hair flowed in the warm night air. Her mother appeared no older than herself. If they'd been standing side by side, they could easily be mistaken for sisters. Well, except they didn't really look anything alike.

Tara's blonde hair and green eyes were the opposite of her mother's darker hair and deep brown eyes.

"Mom? Where is Selene?" she asked. Each time her mother had appeared to her, she had asked for more information on her sisters' whereabouts. Every single time, her mother had skirted her questions.

"She'll find you soon enough," her mother responded. "When it's time."

"Is Typhon really my father?" she asked. Her mother nodded. "What about my dad? What about Jason Dawson?" she asked as her heart broke a little for the man who had loved and raised her.

"One of the many mortals I've loved. I thought it best to leave you with him, knowing you would be safe. I hated deceiving him and letting him believe that you were his, but he served his purpose," her mother said with a shrug.

"Is that what you did with Selene?" Tara asked. "Is she with another one of your… unsuspecting exploits?"

"She is not the chosen one." Her mother shrugged.

"Chosen?" Tara shook her head. "What does that mean?"

Instead of answering, her mother smiled. "Selene is somewhere that she was able to grow up safely," her mother responded.

"On this Earth?" Tara asked. Her mother's dark eyebrow rose slightly.

Her mother shrugged. "Worlds are no more than a reflection."

"What does that even mean?" she asked.

Her mother smiled. "Soon enough, daughter, you will have the answers you seek."

As with each time her mother had visited her, the darkness started to surround them and before she could blink, the vision of her mother was gone. She felt Colt's warm breath on her neck as the feeling of his arms surrounding her allowed her to relax back into sleep.

As she showered and dressed the following morning, she ran everything over in her mind. It was less than five days before the Harvest Moon, when her mother would be there.

She had assumed that was when her father would be there also. Maybe they had more time? Maybe her mother was coming to help them?

Something deep inside her told her that wasn't the case. She doubted her mother was evil, like Typhon was, but still, she was having a difficult time trusting the woman who had abandoned her.

Over the last week, she'd slowly let her guard down. Even though she was having nightly nightmares about her parents and the coming darkness overtaking the world, being around Colt and the others had allowed her to feel safe.

At least she wasn't in this alone.

She'd come a long way from the naive girl in the princess dress living in a castle on the hill. When she'd been growing up, she would have never been caught trucking through the woods or sleeping in a van. She'd had a canopy bed with silk sheets and had strolled through expensive shops, spending her father's money.

"Getting lost in thought?" Colt asked her as she pulled on her hiking boots.

She smiled up at him. "I was just thinking about how much has changed in my life."

He sat next to her on the bed. "This life or since all the others?" he said, nudging her shoulder.

She chuckled. "This one." She rested her head on his shoulder. "You wouldn't think of it to look at me now, but I was raised with extreme privilege."

"Oh?" He glanced down at her. "I can still see some princess in there." He tapped her nose playfully.

She sat up and turned towards him. "My mother left me there. To be raised by…"

"Your father," he broke in. "From what you've told me of the man, he was a loving, caring man who loved you and made sure you had everything you ever wanted growing up."

She was silent for a moment, thinking. "Do you think he's still out there? Wondering what happened to me?" she asked.

Over the years she'd pushed that question, those thoughts, to the back of her mind. She would be heartbroken to know that he'd been searching for her. That she'd been the one who had disappeared that day in front of everyone. After all, she'd been the one who had been whisked away to another Earth, not everyone else and not her home.

Was it still sitting on the hill, overlooking a town that was not in this world? Were her dad and stepmother searching everywhere for her, heartbroken about the daughter they had lost?

"Hey." Colt wrapped his arms around her and held onto her. "When this is all over, maybe we can find a way back to them," he suggested. "After all, Joleen was able to go between worlds."

"Yeah," she said with a sigh. "You're right." She felt a little better. "I'd like that." She looked into his eyes and touched his cheek. "Exploring different worlds with you."

 *E*ach moment he got to spend with Tara, his feelings for her grew. Since that night they'd toasted and he'd seen his past with her, his dreams were filled with more images of their past lives together, glimpses into the lives they had shared. How their love had bloomed and grown into something so big, it allowed them to find each other in the beyond.

Each day when Tara worked, he sat in the coffee shop and researched all he could on… well, everything.

Currently, he was focused on Typhon, Tara's father. Not only had he allegedly fathered some of the scariest monsters in mythology, but he had also created Cerberus, the three-headed hound of hell, possibly one of the scariest beasts in mythology.

Colt read all the myths about how he'd tried to overthrow Zeus but had been defeated by the god's thunderbolts. He wondered vaguely if Tara knew how to throw lightning. He could just imagine her standing in her hiking boots, worn jeans, and flannel coat, holding a bolt of lightning between her hands as her blonde hair flowed around. For good measure, he had her skin glowing like it had several times when he'd pleased her.

"What are you smiling about?" someone asked. He glanced up to see Jacob sliding into the seat across from him.

"Just imaging this is Tara." He turned his computer screen around and showed Jacob the drawing of Zeus holding his thunderbolt.

Jacob laughed. "I think you think too highly of your woman."

"She's not mine to have," he said softly. "Not yet at any rate."

"Oh, I'd say the two of you are totally gone for one another." Jacob leaned forward. "Trust me. As a man who is totally gone for his wife, we tend to recognize one another."

Colt smiled. "No kid today?" he asked, glancing around the coffee shop.

"He's with Auntie Xtina. I'm heading into the office and just wanted to stop off for a quick pick-me-up," he said moments before Jess set a cup and a blueberry muffin in front of Jacob. Jess kissed him quickly and then disappeared back behind the counter. "I love being married to a witch," Jacob said under his breath.

"It probably does come with some perks." He glanced over to where Tara was busy making a cappuccino.

"What about dating the strongest woman alive. Oh, and one that can fly. I bet that's fun," Jacob said after taking a sip of his drink.

"It does have some perks," he said with a grin.

"Well." Jacob started to get up.

"I had a quick question, if you have a moment?" Colt asked.

"Sure." Jacob sat back down. "Shoot."

"What happened to all of you..." he started.

"Which time?" Jacob asked.

"The last time, with Thanatos," he added, trying not to let any of the other guests overhear them.

"Right." Jacob motioned for him to go on.

"Liz mentioned she'd gotten help from another god," Colt said.

"Hypnos," Jacob added quietly. "I'm not one-hundred-percent sure the guy was good. He scared…" He stopped and shook his head. "Liz was positive that if it hadn't been for him, we wouldn't have been able to send the rest of them back."

"Right." Colt glanced down at his screen again.

"What's all this about?" Jacob asked.

"Rhea," he said, nodding towards Tara. "If she really is her mother and, according to everything that I could find on her, a good being, then maybe she's coming to help with… what's coming. Whatever that is."

"Typhon," Jacob said, shaking his head. "Sounds like one nasty being. Something tells me the man isn't going to be alone."

"Right." Colt hadn't really thought of that. Typhon was the father of monsters. Surely, he had a few of them trailing along for the ride.

"Now I've scared you," Jacob added with a sigh.

"No, just presented another challenge. That's all."

"Good." Jacob stood suddenly and slapped Colt on the shoulder. "Keep looking at life like that and you might just survive the week." He chuckled as he picked up his coffee and his muffin. "See you later."

"See you," Colt said, looking back down at his screen. Okay, he thought, time to figure out what sort of monsters could be heading their way.

For the next two hours, he read myth after myth. He flipped through drawings, paintings, and descriptions of the monsters that Typhon had supposedly created. At least the ones that the ancient Greeks had taken notice of.

The most notable was Cerberus, who was, if myths can be trusted, still guarding the gates of hell.

But the thing that bothered Colt the most was that Typhon was in some places labeled as a Titan, like Rhea was, not a god. Titans were bad, worse than most gods. Why had Rhea and Typhon created a child? How was that even possible if Typhon was really a giant with snakes as legs and dragons and snakes as fingers?

The best description he could find of Rhea was that she was a beautiful goddess. She was often depicted holding a staff or a baby, since she was the mother of gods.

In one image, she was holding the staff and a crown while riding a lion. In the sky was a crescent moon and a bright star.

When he did a little more research, he found out that the Nemean Lion was a legendary creature. Its fur was impenetrable by the weapons of humans, making it virtually unstoppable.

What caught his attention was that the lion itself was described as a child of Typhon. So far, the drawing was the only thing he'd found that had linked Rhea to Typhon.

The closer they got to when Rhea was to arrive, the more frustrated and desperate he grew. He supposed he was grasping at straws at this point.

"What has such a big frown on your face?" Jess asked as she refilled his water glass.

He motioned for her to sit and waited until she took the spot across from him.

"Tell me your group has an ace up their sleeve?" he said in a low tone so that Tara wouldn't hear.

Jess sighed. "It's not necessarily an ace, but we do have each other. We've successfully gotten out of worse pickles."

"Right." He nodded. "Okay, so, there's power in the numbers."

Jess nodded. "There has been from the start of things." She leaned closer. "Besides, I wouldn't worry too much about our girl there." She nodded towards Tara, who happened to glance over and look at them at that exact time. "She can lift a piano and fly. Who knows what other tricks she has up her sleeve?" Jess winked at him and stood up to go clear a couple tables.

He thought about Jess's words as he helped them clean up and close the shop later that day.

They still had half the day to themselves before everyone else could meet and had yet to decide what to do with the rest of their time. As Jess was locking up, Tara came over to him and suggested they head back to the hotel for a few hours of rest.

He could see the weariness in her eyes, so he drove them back down the street to their hotel.

"Tired?" he asked her when they stepped into the room.

"No, just… restless. I wanted some time to talk before we met the others later." She moved over and sat on the edge of the bed.

"Okay." He walked over and sat next to her. "What about?"

"Us," she said plainly.

Here it comes, he thought. Everything they had seen, everything she'd seen and told him about, most likely had finally caught up with them. He'd been doubting that she planned to stick around after she'd explained how he'd been the reason for each and every one of her demises.

"Okay," he said a little slower.

She took his hand in hers. "Not that. I'm not… breaking things off with you," she finished, and he relaxed slightly.

"Good, because"—he lifted her hands to his lips—"I really enjoy the taste of you."

She smiled. "And I haven't finished with you either."

"What then?" he asked as she turned a little more serious.

"It's about… my parents." She stood up and walked over to the nightstand and pulled out a notepad. "It's everything I can remember from the dreams," she said as she handed it to him. "I know you've been researching them. Maybe this will help." She sat back down next to him. "If you want, we can go over what you have so far, you know, to see if anything… jogs something loose." She tapped the side of her head.

He pulled out his computer and set it on the small table by the window. He opened the software where he had all of the research so far.

"Wow, you've got a lot in here," she said, looking over his shoulder. He moved over and pulled the other chair next to his.

Going over everything that he'd found out about her parents, about what she was, somehow was more difficult than reading it himself. Somehow, telling her all of the details made it a little more… real.

"Jess thinks there's more to you than the powers you've shown us," he said. "I know firsthand that you light up like a night-light," he added with a smile.

She chuckled. "Only when I'm happy and good emotions are spiking."

"Right." His smile slipped a little. "Is there more?"

The way she bit her bottom lip and looked worried assured him there was.

Instead of answering, she glanced down at her watch. "We have another hour before we're supposed to meet everyone. What do you say we go for a drive?"

Nodding, he shut down his computer and motioned for her to lead the way. When she grabbed her coat, he took his jacket, figuring whatever she wanted to show him would be outside.

"Want to drive?" he asked, holding up his keys, which she took easily from him.

For the next ten minutes, he sat in his passenger seat and watched the dull gray countryside pass by him.

In the week and a half since they'd arrived in town, most of the colorful fall leaves had fallen. Now, the leaves were in heaps on the ground, soggy, dull, and forgotten, leaving the countryside bare and boring.

When she parked, he realized she intended to go to the field near the silo.

"Are you sure about this?" he asked.

"Yes, it has to be here." She looked out at the mist that covered the hay field.

He wanted to ask her what, but she was already getting out of the truck. He followed her for a while, through the tall wet hay until they stopped near the middle of the open field.

"She was here. They were both here," she whispered.

"Who? Your parents?" He stood beside her. She nodded, while keeping her eyes on the horizon. "It was sunny and warm." She closed her eyes. "They met here."

"Met?" he asked, looking around. Whatever he'd imagined about two gods meeting and hooking up, it hadn't been in a field in the middle of nowhere Georgia.

"Yes," she said with a sigh. "This place, the land, it holds power." She lifted her arms and he watched in amazement as she rose off the ground until she floated effortlessly almost a hundred feet above him.

As he stood there, under her, he saw a pulse of air shoot out from her in a circular motion. It created a wave that eventually dissipated at the horizon.

When her feet touched the ground again, he asked. "What was that?"

"A call."

"To?" he asked, noticing a change in her eyes.

"Selene," she said. "I thought I'd at least try, if she's on this world. Since there's more power here, I figured it would boost my signal."

He wrapped his arms around her. "Is this the power you wanted to show me?" he asked.

She reached up on her toes, kissed him briefly, then dropped her arms and stood back. "No, this is." She smiled briefly before vanishing completely in front of his eyes.

"Tara?" he asked, glancing around him.

"Still here." Her voice came from directly behind him. When he turned, she was standing there.

"Teleportation?" he asked.

She shook her head. "Invisibility."

His smile grew. "Wicked."

"No." She shook her head. "Not necessarily. When I use this power…" She frowned slightly. "It's hard to describe. It's like I slip into a different realm. One over this one. Yet somehow filled with…" He saw her shiver as she wrapped her arms around her. "I think it's Tartarus."

"Hell?" he asked, aghast.

She nodded and looked down at her hands. "The first time I discovered it, I didn't realize I'd turned invisible. I had to record myself to find that out. The other thing about that power is that it's as if the world continues to turn without me. When I reappear, I'm never in the exact place I had been when I'd disappeared. Close but never in the exact spot."

"It's why you were behind me instead of in front of me?" he asked, glancing up at the sun to ensure the theory.

"Yes." She nodded. "When I discovered this, I had to hike almost a full mile back to where I was staying."

"I guess it's handy if you need to escape?" he suggested.

"If you don't mind a short trip to hell," she added. "It doesn't freak you out?"

"Why would it?" he asked, noticing the worry behind her eyes.

Instead of answering, she shook her head and took a deep breath. "You amaze me."

He laughed. "You're the one who can fly, has super strength, and can turn invisible. Why on earth do I amaze you?"

She walked back over to him, once again putting her arms around his shoulders. "Because you take all this in and, each time I show you something scary, you smile and look at me as if it's the most amazing thing in the world instead of freaking out and running for the hills. You're not out here· taking pictures and trying to expose me as a freak. You just…"—she shrugged slightly— "accept me."

He winced when she mentioned pictures. After all, he had an amazing picture of her at the top of the silo with the moon in the background that he hadn't told her about.

He sighed heavily. "I did take one picture," he admitted, pulling out his cell phone. "For my eyes only." He handed her the phone. "You can delete it if you want."

She looked down at his screen and, to his amazement, she smiled and then laughed. "That is a really great shot." She handed him the phone again. "Trust me, if anyone other than the group saw it, they'd believe it was a fake."

He looked at the image and smiled. "You are pretty amazing." He tucked the phone away, then pulled her into his arms. "I don't think there's anything you could do that would make me think otherwise."

He felt her relax in his arms. "I used to wish I was normal. I mean, growing up I didn't have any of these powers. I think the world my mother left me on somehow blocked out my powers." She glanced up at the sky. Even though it was dusk, she could see the moon hovering in the sky over the field. "I don't know if that has something to do with it, but I'm beginning to think it does. My world had two moons, not one."

"I've been thinking about that," he said, but then he glanced down at his watch. "I want the others to hear my theory, and we're going to be late if we don't head on over to Mike and Xtina's place."

She stopped him from walking back to his truck by taking his hands. "Colt, I never expected to find someone… who would accept me. Then you came along, and we discover that we've been connected…"

"Forever," he added with a smile.

She nodded. "I never imagined I'd be so lucky as to find you again." She lifted on her toes and kissed him. "I guess what I'm trying to say is… I love you."

Colt felt his heart skip a beat and then burst with joy. He'd never felt this way about anyone before. Never imagined he'd find anyone like Tara, anyone as unique and amazing. He knew without a doubt what he felt for her and easily allowed those feelings to flow from him as he pulled her into his arms and kissed her, making a point to tell her just how he felt.

ara couldn't contain her joy as she and Colt walked through Xtina and Mike's front door. She hadn't planned on making love to Colt in the field where she herself had been conceived.

Then again, she hadn't known that bit of information when she'd followed the call of power as she'd driven to the location in the first place.

Ever since she'd found out about her sister, she'd been trying to reach her power out to find her. Sensing the power at the field, she'd tried once more. She hadn't known she'd shot out a wave of power until Colt had explained it as he drove to Xtina and Mike's place.

"What did it look like?" she asked, curious.

"I should have videoed it," he said with a shake of his head. He glanced over at her. "For scientific purposes. I bet the others would have liked to see it, as well. Would you have minded? I know with your past..."

"I trust you," she said, taking his hand in hers as he parked next to Jacob's patrol car. "If you want or need to, you have my permission."

Colt nodded. "I'll keep that in mind next time."

Half an hour later, they sat around the dining room table, munching on snacks as everyone chatted amongst themselves.

"I have a theory I'd like to run by everyone," Colt said, getting everyone's attentions.

"About?" Jess asked.

"Why Rhea chose the world she did to leave Tara on." He glanced at her. "Tara's mentioned that where she was raised, on her home world, there were two moons instead of one. Has anyone heard of the giant-impact theory?"

"You're talking about the theory that the moon was formed during a collision between the Earth and another small planet. The moon was created from debris collected in Earth's orbit," Mason said.

"Right." Colt nodded.

"So, what? Where Tara came from, this process didn't form one moon, but two?" Xtina asked.

"You think that had something to do with why Rhea chose that planet?" Jess asked.

"You all mentioned it before when describing what happened with Thanatos. His prison is up there." Colt pointed up.

"Along with my mother," Jess added.

"Tara mentioned earlier that there is power in places." Colt looked towards her. "There must be power up there to hold Thanatos and your mother," he said to Jess.

"Right," Jess agreed and visibly shivered.

"You think I didn't have my powers until I came here because of the moons? Because I grew up under two moons instead of one?" Tara asked.

"Their power was split." Colt nodded. "It's at least a theory." He shrugged.

"A good one," Mason added. "If you think about it, a

battery needs a negative and positive connection in the same physical unit to work. If one of your two moons was positive and one was negative, but they never touched…"

"No power," Tara said. "In her way, I think she left me there to protect me. If I didn't have my power, maybe Typhon couldn't find me?"

"So, from the moment you stepped foot on this planet or realm, whatever"—Xtina shrugged— "you've been hunted?"

"Maybe?" Tara answered. "But then why did my mother have to hire Colt to find me?"

Everyone turned towards Colt. "Maybe she already knew where you were. I mean, she did tell me the time and place where you would be to start following you. If she knew about us, about our past together, then just maybe she was using this as an excuse to get us together?"

"That's possible," Tara agreed. "And not a day has gone by in the past two weeks that I don't thank her for it," she said taking his hand in hers.

"Ditto," Colt said with a smile.

"There's power in connections and love," Jess broke in. "Maybe she knows you'll need that power to fight what is coming?"

Tara smiled over at Colt, remembering how wonderful it felt to tell him how she felt. For the first time since she'd come to this world, she was free to open her feelings. To be free. Even that had new power pulsing through her veins.

"So, any idea what is coming?" Brea asked.

"Typhon, which brings the darkness," Tara answered, her smile slipping.

"How do we combat darkness? I mean," Jess started, "with a really big lightbulb?"

Colt turned to her and motioned. "Show them."

Tara frowned. "Show them what exactly?"

"How you can combat the darkness." Colt smiled his encouragement at her.

She had never thought to use that power in such a way before. After all, it wasn't one of her cooler powers. It was just… more of an annoyance really.

"Do you have something that we can use to fight this?" Xtina asked.

"It's not… I mean, yes, if it works, but it's not really… reliable." She shook her head. "I have to… feel…" She closed her eyes, feeling totally stupid.

"Here," Colt said, taking her hand and pulling her up into his arms. "Bear with us," he told the group. Then he bent his head down and kissed her.

At first, she tensed. She wasn't really into putting on a show. But then his mouth slanted over hers and she lost focus on time and place. More importantly, who was watching.

She wouldn't have noticed the moment her powers started if not for the group's gasps that filled the room.

When Colt broke the connection, he was smiling at her with pride.

"Radiant," he said, his eyes on hers.

"Show off." She nudged him.

"I have so many questions," Mason said, causing several people to chuckle.

"How long can you hold it?" Jess asked.

"Until we break the connection." She held up her and Colt's joined hands, then dropped her hand from his. Instantly, she felt her power drain and the room grew dimmer.

"Okay, so our first play is to keep the two of you together for as long as possible," Jacob added.

"Do you have any other powers you've been hiding?" Jess asked, a gleam in her eyes.

She glanced around the room and knew instantly that the group was counting on her. If she was going to save this world, she needed to trust them.

"Yes, but I don't like showing you inside. Too many variables." She glanced around.

"Let's carry the party out to the back," Mike suggested.

"You go, I'll stay with the kids," Xtina added. "It's time for Harper's dinner."

Everyone except for Xtina filed out the back door and stood around Tara as she willed her other power to carry her to Tartarus.

Normally, when she went to the other realm, it was dark, filled with the smells of sulfur and soot. Clouds of mist bellowed around, blocking out any light, and sounds of screaming and agony filled her ears. This time, however, everything was still. A river of lava flowed to the left of her as a blinding light shone in the distance, almost a beacon in the darkness.

Instantly, she knew something was wrong.

"To what do I owe a visit twice in one day, daughter?" The hissing voice sounded almost directly behind her.

She spun around and fully saw the creature that was her father for the first time.

He was indeed tall. His entire body filled her vision. Snakes crawled all over his body. She could understand why myths had his body made of the things. They were everywhere, like a suit of armor. Only his face was clear of the slithering creatures. He was a handsome enough man, and she saw no resemblance between them.

She recoiled at the sound of a million snakes hissing and slithering around his body. His legs did appear to be made of snakes, as in all the descriptions. She figured it was the snakes working in unison that kept him upright.

Her first instinct was to leave and quickly return to safety and to the others.

When Typhon chuckled, she stilled. "I think I'll keep you here for a while. There are some things we need to discuss."

"Are you really my father?" she asked.

"Yes, little goddess, I am," he hissed.

"Why do you call me a goddess?"

"It's what you are. I am a god, your mother is a goddess, therefore you are one too." He pointed to his chest and, for a moment, she saw a hand under the snakes. So, he was humanoid under all the reptiles.

"I thought all gods were bad?" she asked.

He chuckled. "That's like saying all humans are bad." He shook his head. "You shouldn't believe everything you read."

She glanced around her. "Then why are you locked away here?" she asked, motioning to their surroundings.

"Who says I'm locked here?" he asked. "Have not some of your Earth's history books gotten facts wrong?"

She thought about it and nodded slowly. "So, you aren't the father of all monsters?" she asked.

"That I am, daughter. Unfortunately. But you, you are something special. Something I have been waiting and hoping for since the dawn of time."

She stood in front of him, silent, running over the information he was giving her.

"My mother?" she asked.

"Is complicated," Typhon answered. "The only thing I can tell you is that you can't trust a god. Like I said, not all of us are what we seem."

She could feel the pull of reality drawing her back to Colt and the others.

"Remember that, my little goddess, when she comes for you." Typhon's voice echoed as she phased back to the real world. She stood more than twenty yards from the spot she'd been previously. She could hear everyone calling for her as they searched the backyard.

"Here," she called out. "I'm here." She walked around the house from the front driveway.

"She's here," Colt said as he rushed to her and wrapped his arms up. "You were gone a while," he said into her hair. "We were worried."

"Wow, what a neat trick," Jess said rushing towards them. "Colt explained what it was while you were MIA."

"What happened?" Colt asked her.

"I had a little chat with my father," she answered. "Why don't we head inside so I can fill everyone in on the conversation?"

It was good to be back. Part of her wanted to believe what Typhon had said. About him and about her mother.

As she filled everyone in on what he had said, however, they all came to the agreement that no god could be trusted, no matter what the history books or myths said.

"So where does this leave us?" Colt asked after they were done discussing what had happened to her.

"Pretty much back where we started," Jess said with a yawn. "And now it's time for bed." She looked at her watch. "Until tomorrow." She picked up her sleeping son from the little pop-up crib where Reed and Harper had fallen asleep together while the adults talked.

It was strange. Since the day so long ago that she'd first discovered herself in a new world, with abilities beyond her imagination, she'd never hoped for any sort of normalcy. Never dreamed that she'd find a man who would accept her for what she was. Let alone think of having her own family.

Now, watching the two families shelter and love their children, she started dreaming. Started wondering what it would be like to settle down with Colt.

They'd make the cutest kids together. Maybe they would

have his dark hair and his haunting hazel eyes. Would Colt want to settle here in Hidden Creek or head back up to Seattle where his mother still lived?

She'd never imagined she'd live in the south, but she didn't want to leave her new friends. Not when it was possible that they were the only ones in the world that understood what she was going through.

Could she afford to let her guard down and really start hoping for a brighter future? She doubted the peace would last. It was only two days now before her mother arrived.

When she'd first found out, she'd been excited to meet the woman. The goddess. Now, she wasn't so sure. Was that what Typhon had wanted? To put doubt in her mind about Rhea. Why? Was it all part of a game?

That night when she fell asleep in Colt's arms, she slept for the first time in days without a visit from either of her parents. Instead, she dreamed of a white house on a hill with blue shutters and picture windows that overlooked a green field. There was a picket fence circling the house and a smaller yard that held a swing set. Two brown dogs ran around chasing one another as Colt laughed and played with two small boys of about five years old, both of whom looked just like him. Tara sat on the back porch, swinging and singing softly to a small girl no more than a year old. The girl's blonde curly hair caught the last rays of the summer sun and shone brightly as her little green eyes smiled up at her.

CHAPTER 16

It was as if coming face to face with her father in hell had been a good thing for Tara. On the day after the incident, Tara was in a better mood than he'd witnessed before.

She seemed to almost hum when she talked and he noticed with a great deal of pleasure that she had an extra swing to her step.

Whatever had gone on between her and her father that she hadn't shared with the group had put her in good spirits. Maybe it was that, no matter what, come tomorrow there would be more answers. Or maybe she was just trying to have the best last full day of her life before the chaos ensued. Whatever the reason, he wasn't going to be the one to put a damper on her spirits.

Instead of sitting in the Coffee Corner while she worked her morning shift, he headed into town to get a few things and to make a private phone call.

He figured it was high time he called his mother. He'd talked to her two weeks ago, when he'd been on the road, and had told her where he was and roughly how long he planned on being gone. But seeing as the world might be ending in a day, he figured he ought to talk to her one last time.

He'd thought about warning her of the Earth's impending doom, but then figured she'd think he'd gone crazy, or he'd joined one of those end of days cults. Either way, he didn't want her to freak out. Besides, he knew that the group might be able to fight what was coming and save the day. After all, with all the stories from the past two years that the group had told them, there was a slight chance things might go a different direction.

Slight. But still a chance.

"Hey, Mom," he said when his mother answered the phone on the fourth ring. She had most likely forgotten the last place where she'd left her phone and had been desperately rushing around to find.

"Hey," she responded a little breathless. "Sorry, I left my phone in the bathroom."

He chuckled. "You need one of those chain thingies on your cell phone like you wear on your glasses, so you don't lose it," he joked.

"I'm sure you didn't call me just to remind me how forgetful I am," she joked back.

It was one of the things he loved about the woman. Even in the face of darkness, she always had her humor intact.

"No, I'm just checking in. Making sure everything is okay up there." He shifted in his truck seat as he sat outside the local grocery store. He planned to run in and grab something nice for just the two of them for dinner. Jess had mentioned during breakfast that the group had decided to take a reprieve for the last night. He also planned to grab some flowers for Tara.

They had never officially gone out on a date, so he wanted to make the night as special as he could.

"Where are you now?" his mother asked.

"Hidden Creek, Georgia," he responded easily. "Small southern town doesn't begin to describe it. It's nice. Homey," he thought out loud.

"Oh, good. I've never been to Georgia," his mother told him. "Are you going to be there long?"

"I might," he answered. "Mom, I met the one."

All his life, his mother had warned him that when he met the one, the woman he would care for as much as she had cared for his dad, he would know.

"Ohhh," his mother said, giggling. "Now I know I have to plan a trip. I'm getting online right now and looking for tickets."

"Hang on," he said, smiling. "We might come up your way. At least… well, I guess we haven't really planned for anything yet."

"Okay, tell me everything," his mother said, sounding eager.

For the next fifteen minutes, he told his mother all that he could about Tara, without adding any of the crazy stuff.

By the time he got off the phone, he was pretty sure his mother was planning his and Tara's wedding.

After hanging up the phone, he spent the next twenty minutes walking through the grocery store, trying to plan out a special dinner. It was hard to do when their hotel room only had a microwave and a small refrigerator.

There had been a point in his life where he'd believed he wanted to go to culinary school. Maybe even open his own restaurant. Having been raised in a family that owned their own bakery, he'd gained a love of cooking and baking at an early age.

He may not be able to make the meal he wanted for Tara tonight, but still, he came out on top with a nice salad and some quality premade meals from the deli area. He followed that up with a bottle of champagne and a pretty awesome-looking chocolate fudge brownie from the bakery, along with a small container of ice cream. Thankfully, as he was checking out, he remembered the flowers and grabbed a beautiful bouquet of purple tulips.

After dropping everything off at their hotel room and setting the stage for the evening, he drove back to the coffee shop and waited for her shift to be over.

He had never been as nervous for a first date as he was now. His palms started sweating as he watched Tara happily working behind the counter.

"You've got this," Jess said, walking over to his table and setting a cup of coffee down in front of him. "You'll need the extra energy." She winked and then walked away.

He was growing accustomed to being friends with a witch. He doubted he would be able to go back to being around anyone normal after this.

"Someone's in a good mood," Tara said when he started helping them clean and lock up the coffee shop.

"Just happy we finally have an evening to ourselves." He took her hand and spun her around the floor in a dance move his mother had taught him back in junior high for his first dance.

Tara's laughter rang out in the empty shop. "Sexy, strong, and dances," she joked. "It'll be fun discovering what other skills you have." She practically purred, and he felt his desire for her grow.

"I can cook," he added in stupidly. "I need a kitchen, but…" He shrugged, trying not to sound stupid.

"Maybe soon you can cook for me." She sighed as she walked into his arms. "I've always liked cooking. It was important to have a good kitchen area in my van."

"I still don't get how you lived in such a small space." He shook his head.

"I'm not over six feet tall and as wide as a tree trunk," she joked. "And since it was just me for so long, it was easier than paying for a place of my own." She went back to flipping chairs up onto the tables.

"What are your plans after… tomorrow?" he asked, helping her with the chairs.

She glanced over at him and shrugged. "I don't think I've really thought too much about it." She glanced around and a slight smile formed on her lips. "I kind of like Hidden Creek. I mean, the people understand me. I like working here," she added as she finished with the last chair. He walked over and stood beside her. "It feels… right." She looked at him.

"Yeah." He nodded. "I talked to my mother earlier. She really wants to come down here for a visit."

Her eyebrows rose. "So you're planning on sticking around here then?"

He nudged her shoulder. "If you are, I am."

Her smile doubled. "Maybe we can look for someplace other than a hotel then?"

He nodded. "I was thinking. I know you haven't tried my cooking yet, but since I doubt there's enough business for someone like me in such a small town, I might try my hand at opening my own place."

She looked at him in surprise. "You want to open your own restaurant?"

"I've been thinking about it. Actually, it's been in the back of my mind since high school. I took a few classes after I got out of the military, but sort of just slipped into security since the last thing Seattle needed was another restaurant." He glanced out the front windows. "I think Hidden Creek might be able to handle one. What do you think?"

"I think it's a great idea," Jess said from behind him. They both turned to see Jess leaning against the counter. "Sorry, eavesdropping is one of my superpowers." She smiled.

"There's a perfect building for lease just down the street. It used to be a café until the owner's wife died. It's been up for sale for over a year. I know the owner is highly motivated at this point to get it off his hands."

Colt glanced over at Tara, who nodded.

"We have the rest of the day off. If you want to schedule with the owner to have a look at it, I'm game," Tara said.

He turned to Jess with a smile. "Can you arrange a meeting?"

Jess laughed as she pulled out her phone.

Less than fifteen minutes later, they met the owner, Daryl Cox, at the building two blocks away from the Coffee Corner. From the outside, Colt could tell instantly that the place was perfect.

It was an old two-story brick building that had a wide covered front porch on the main floor. Above was an exposed balcony. The entire front of the building on the main floor was windows.

Before the owner arrived, he and Tara peeked inside the windows. It had old wood floors that just needed a little sanding and a fresh coat of lacquer. There was a long bar along one of the interior brick walls. Old lights hung overhead, which he instantly thought of replacing with new modern looking ones.

"With a little work, this place would be perfect," Tara said as she cupped her hands and glanced into the windows.

"Yeah. Let's just hope there's a kitchen in the back," Colt added.

"I wonder what's upstairs?" Tara said, standing back and looking up at the deck area.

Just then a car pulled up and parked next to his truck. When a large black man stepped out, he went and shook the man's hand. It was strange, but ex-military tended to know one another.

"Armed services?" Daryl asked as he shook Colt's hand.

Colt nodded. "Four years in special ops. You?"

"Eight," the man said with a smile.

For the next few minutes, they talked about their service. Then Daryl pulled out a key ring and opened the front door.

"There's a fully equipped kitchen in the back. You might need a new dishwasher, but the rest of it was updated last year," he said, stepping inside.

Colt's mind filled with images of tables, booths, bar stools, and people enjoying the space.

Tara followed him to the back and the moment they walked into the kitchen, he knew it was perfect for what he wanted.

"What's upstairs?" Tara asked.

"An apartment," Daryl answered. "I've been trying to rent the place out to make a little money, but no luck so far. Are you two looking for a place to stay?"

"We've been thinking about it," Colt answered, looking at Tara. "Want to take a look?"

She nodded, and they followed Daryl out the back door, climbed the inside stairs, and walked into a two-bedroom apartment with a large living room and a smaller kitchen space. Windows looked out over the small town. French doors opened up to the balcony out front.

"It's... so big," Tara said with a chuckle.

"Everything's bigger than your van." He walked over to her and wrapped his arms around her.

"I'll give you two a few moments to discuss it," Daryl said. "I'll be downstairs."

"What do you think?" Colt asked her.

"I like it," Tara said, but he could see a little worry in her eyes.

"Problems?" he asked.

"It's just…" She shrugged. "I've never lived with someone before. I don't know if I'll be any good at it."

He chuckled. "I haven't either. I guess we'll find out together."

She tilted her head. "I mean, how do we do this? Pool our resources together?"

"We can figure that out in due time. I have enough in savings for a down payment. The rest…" He shrugged. "We'll figure it out. If you're willing?"

She wrapped her arms around his shoulder. "The world may end tomorrow. Anything beyond that is just a bonus. If I get to spend that time with you, then I'd happily do it anywhere." She reached up on her toes and kissed him.

"Great. Let's go make Daryl an offer," he said eagerly.

CHAPTER 17

Tara had never been given flowers before. Nor had she had anyone make her dinner. When they returned to their hotel room after signing the paperwork on the building, she walked into the room and saw the romantic setting Colt had prepared for their evening.

"Wow," she said, stepping inside. "You did all this?"

"I figure that if we're going to live together, we might as well have a first date," he joked, handing her a bouquet of purple tulips.

"Do you know," she said as she buried her face in the flowers, "that we didn't have tulips where I came from?"

"Seriously?" he asked, giving her a look of astonishment.

She laughed. "No, of course we had tulips." She nudged his shoulder playfully and enjoyed the sound of his laughter.

"Okay, now I want to know everything that is different between our universes," he said as he pulled out the chair for her. "Did you have Nazis, Cleopatra, the *Titanic*?"

"Yes, to all. Since I've been here, I've tried to find all the contrasts. I'd say the biggest differences are that we didn't drop any atomic bombs and that our music is far better than yours."

He set an elaborate salad down in front of her. It looked better than anything she'd ever eaten. There were strawberries, blueberries, walnuts, and cheese on top of crisp green lettuce.

"I highly doubt that. I mean, did you have Elvis?" Colt asked.

"Yeah." She nodded. "He's still singing and officiating over weddings in Vegas."

He chuckled. "We have that too. Are you sure it's the real Elvis?" He sat across from her.

"Oh, he's the real one," she answered with a smile. "At least my Elvis is still alive… which makes this a seriously screwed-up version of the universe." Again, his warm laughter filled her heart.

For the next hour, as he fed her, she tried to elicit it as much as she could. They laughed about a few more small differences between their worlds.

Whatever happened the next day, at least they'd had today to laugh and love. She wanted to make sure that their last time together was perfect.

Neither of them brought up the next day. Instead, she listened to Colt dream about opening his own restaurant and bar. They talked about what would be needed to fix the place up. About what furniture they would buy for their own apartment. When they were going to move in.

She really liked that Colt was open to her ideas about the restaurant. At first he was just thinking of being open for dinner, but then she mentioned how it would be nice to open a little early for lunch and offer salads, soups, and sandwiches. Then they could have the more elaborate meals for dinnertime.

She didn't know who made the move once the last of the

dinner was finished, but she ended up sitting in his lap. She melted against his chest as his lips covered hers.

Her fingers tangled in his hair, which she noted was longer than it had been two weeks previously. Actually, so much had changed in that short time.

When she'd driven into town, she'd been alone, desperate for answers. Now she had more friends than she'd ever had in her previous life. Friends she trusted with her secrets and her life.

She was settling down and she was in love. She was moving in with Colt and looking forward to helping him start his own business. Commitments had never been her forte before. Now, she didn't even question her future.

If they survived what was coming, she knew without a doubt that she wanted to be with Colt.

"I love you," Colt said against her skin. He stood up, holding her in his arms as he walked towards the bed.

"I love you," she replied as he laid her down gently. They started removing each other's clothes.

She couldn't stop the tears from slipping from her eyes as he cherished her, raining little kisses all over her heated skin. She felt her entire body vibrate with desire, aching for him, needing him more than she had before.

There was so much she wanted to say to him so that he could understand how much he meant to her. Instead, she showed him as they moved together.

This time when he slipped into her, all her barriers broke free, allowing her power to build. With her release, every ounce of control slipped free, shattering everything she'd held at bay.

Power flowed from her, from them, and the entire room shook as the lights flashed.

"Wow," Colt said against the crook of her breast. "Just… wow."

She chuckled. "I agree. Wow." She sighed and ran her fingers through his hair.

"I need a haircut." He sighed. "Tomorrow I'll..." He stopped, and she felt him tense.

"I like your hair a little longer," she said, breaking into his dark thoughts.

He sat up slightly and looked down at her. "Do we need to talk about tomorrow?"

She'd known it was coming. Knew there were things that had to be said. Sitting up, she pulled on his shirt, the one she'd removed from him earlier, and sat on the edge of the bed while Colt slipped on his jeans and pulled two containers from the fridge.

"This discussion calls for chocolate," he said, glancing at her. "And ice cream."

She watched him scoop some ice cream on each brownie cake.

"You are more than amazing," she said as he handed her the container and a spoon. "You are my world."

"Me or the brownie?" he joked as he sat next to her on the bed.

"Both." She took a bite. "Okay, now I think I can talk about tomorrow." She sighed. "I have this feeling that when my mother comes, things are going to turn bad. Which means, more than likely, she is the one we should fear. Not Typhon."

He nodded. "I think we've all felt that way since your last meeting with your dad."

"Okay, so, why would my mother be acting all sweet and kind?" she asked, taking another bite of the sugary goodness.

"Maybe she needs something from you? Maybe she wants to sway you to her side?"

"Maybe she's just toying with me?" she thought out loud.

"With us," he said, taking her free hand.

Nodding she agreed. "Yes, all of us. Either way, all we can do is wait and see and react as best as we can when she shows up."

"So what you're saying is, there's no use worrying tonight?" he asked with a smile.

"Exactly. There is, however, a reason to talk about what will happen if things do go wrong." She set her brownie down and turned to him. She waited for him to set his brownie down as well and then took his hands in hers. "If something should happen to me."

"Don't say that."

"We're realists, remember? If something does happen, sell my van, open your restaurant. Find love again." She hadn't realized tears were slipping from her eyes until he reached up and brushed the wetness from her cheeks.

"Nothing is going to happen to you. I won't let it." He pulled her into his arms.

"I can't bear to think about something happening to you, or any of the others. The kids." She felt her throat close up. "I won't let Jess, Jacob, Xtina, or Mike put themselves in danger."

"I agree," he said firmly. "So how do we go about fighting what's coming without them? Something tells me that if we tried to do it alone, they'd find us somehow and kick our butts."

She smiled and pulled back slightly to look up at him. "Jess is actually treating the entire ordeal as if it's going to be fun."

"Jacob too." Colt shook his head. "Don't forget, they've done this a few times already. Saved the world from gods and all that."

She smiled. "Okay, so we both agree, we can't do it without them, but we don't want anything to happen to anyone else."

She knew that he understood what she was saying when he nodded slowly. "How do we go about doing that?"

"Joe and Brea might be able to help us with that," she said clearly.

"Let's finish the brownies and get dressed before we call them."

"Sounds like a plan." She took up the brownie again. "If you can make a meal this good without a stove, I can't wait to try your cooking for real."

CHAPTER 18

Coming up with a plan to sneak around and sabotage his new friends just felt wrong. Even though they were doing it for all the right reasons, he still felt guilty about it.

After finishing their dessert and taking a quick shower, they dressed and sent a text message to both Joe and Brea to meet them in secret in the field at eleven that night. Colt made a point to request that neither let anyone else know about the meeting, except for their significant others, who were welcome to tag along for the discussion.

Tara had suggested these couples since she was sure they would be more willing to help.

In the short time they'd been in Georgia, the weather had gone from sweltering heat to rain to almost full-blown chilly fall.

They walked through the muddy field, which used to be planted with tall grain but had in the past few days been plowed. Thankfully, they had brought flashlights to light their way and had worn thick jackets to keep out the chill in the night.

They waited almost ten minutes before Joe appeared quickly with Liz in his arms. By the time he set her down, Brea shimmered next to them, holding onto Ethan's arm.

Everyone was dressed warmly, holding their own flashlights.

"Want to tell us why we're having a private party?" Joe asked, glancing around.

Colt stepped forward. "Tara and I were thinking—"

Tara touched his shoulder, and he stood back and motioned for her to explain.

"There are some sacrifices we aren't willing to make. I've been on my own since I was sixteen. I was shoved into a foster facility and forgotten. We won't let that happen to Reed or Harper or to your unborn child." She motioned to Brea. "We think you both would agree," Tara said, looking at Joe and Brea.

All four of the others nodded in agreement.

"How do we do this?" Brea asked.

"It's going to be tricky, but when things begin," Tara said, "you two will have to coordinate. Brea, I know that you're six months pregnant, which is why, once you've grabbed the others, you and Ethan shouldn't return either."

"Um," Liz said, getting everyone's attention, then looking towards Joe and biting her bottom lip. "I was going to tell you... I just found out yesterday..." Before she said anything further, Joe let out a whooping sound and grabbed his wife up in his arms.

"We're having a baby?" he asked.

Liz laughed and nodded. "We've been trying," she added happily.

"Congratulations," Tara said cheerfully.

"What's in the water around here?" Colt joked as he shook the other two men's hands.

"This leaves just Joleen and Mason," Tara said looking around the group.

"Okay, so all the more reason for the two of you to do your jobs quickly and take off. We doubt any of them will allow us to trick them into not coming…" Colt waited a heartbeat.

"Agreed," everyone said in unison.

"How do we get them away from what's going to happen?" he asked.

"Do we know where? I mean, most likely it's going to be the silo, but are we sure?" Ethan asked, looking towards Tara.

Tara bit her bottom lip and looked at him. "The silo," she confirmed, but Colt could see the lie in her eyes.

He could tell she doubted that there would be any real benefit to having Joleen and Mason there if they were the only ones who could help. It might just be better to not have any of them show up at all. But if not the silo, then where?

"Okay, so we all meet up there at…" Joe asked. "What time?"

"When the full moon rises," Tara answered.

Brea pulled out her phone and, after a moment, answered. "Eight fifty-one tomorrow night," she told them.

"So, at eight thirty, we'll meet there. If I take both Mike and Jacob, Brea can grab Xtina and Jess. We'll take them back to Xtina and Mike's place. They won't have enough time to make it back to the silo before the showdown," Joe suggested.

"Good plan," Colt said, taking Tara's hand. "We'll expect you to stay away. It's our wish," he said motioning to Tara.

"I need your word that you won't try to help. No matter what happens or where things go down." Tara stepped forward. "It matters."

The four of them glanced at one another briefly, then nodded in unison. At that moment, a soft green light radiated from Tara and surrounded them.

"Your word is your bond," she said softly as the light dissipated into the night sky.

"Cool," Joe said. "I could have used that power when I signed the new contract on the house we're building," he joked.

Everyone chuckled.

"We are sorry to take you away from your homes at such a late hour," Tara said. "Thank you for coming."

Just as quickly as they'd arrived, the four of them left again, leaving Tara and Colt standing in the field alone.

"Why did you lie to them?" he asked, glancing down at her. "They made a pact not to help so why tell them to meet at the silo?"

"It's for their own good." She looked up at the stars. "All of them. Even though they made the pact, something tells me they would try to reach us, and I just couldn't take that chance. I wouldn't let them. It's too important."

"I thought we agreed we wouldn't be doing this alone."

Tara was silent for a moment, then she turned towards him. "We won't be." She turned away from him. "Hello, Selene. Sister, why don't you come forward?"

Colt braced and turned towards the darkness where Tara faced.

He shined his flashlight towards the space, only to have it wink out, leaving them in darkness.

"Light won't penetrate darkness," a warm rich voice laced with southern charm said. "And I am the goddess of darkness."

The woman that stepped forward was nothing like he'd imagined Tara's sister to be. She was easily as beautiful as Tara. Her long raven hair lay in intricate braids over each shoulder, and her dark eyes watched them closely.

She was dressed in all black: a pair of pants, a leather jacket, and hiking boots.

"You're Tara," she said, stopping a foot from them. "I've seen you."

"You have?" Tara asked. "This is my first time seeing you." Tara tilted her head, then surprised them both by walking over and wrapping her arms around Selene. "I've always wanted a sister," she said softly.

Selene glanced at him, her eyes going wide as if wondering what was going on. He shrugged and smiled at her.

"I'm Colt," he said, holding out his hand when Tara released her and stepped back.

Selene glanced down at his hand. "Trust me, you do not want me to touch you."

"Okay," he said easily, dropping his hand. Her dark eyes narrowed slightly at that. "When did you get into town?" he asked her.

"A few minutes before your friends left. Nice tricks, by the way," Selene said. "Speedster and..."

"Teleportation," Tara added.

"You?" Colt asked.

Selene's eyes moved to him again. "Something like that."

Tara was quiet and when Selene's gaze landed on her again, she asked, "You've seen me?"

"For about ten years," Selene answered. "The first time you were wearing a ruined prom dress and standing in the rain, crying."

Tara gasped slightly. "The day I arrived."

"Arrived?" Selene asked.

"It's a long story." Tara sighed. "One for a later time."

Selene nodded. "I... couldn't get to you." She frowned and looked down at her hands. "I wanted to help, but..." She shook her head. "I couldn't."

"It's okay." Tara took Selene's hand in her own. Colt noticed the woman jumped slightly at the touch.

Xtina acted the same way around people, and he wondered if she might have a similar situation.

"Are you hungry?" Tara asked.

"No, I'm fine." Selene glanced up at the moon. "I guess the party is tomorrow, huh?"

"Yeah." Tara nodded. "What do you know?"

Selene glanced around. "Got any place a little… warmer we can talk?"

"We've got a hotel room. Where are you staying?" Colt asked Selene.

"A hotel is good. I'll see about getting a room for myself," Selene answered.

"Do you have a car?" Colt asked as they started walking back through the field towards his truck.

"It's back in town," Selene answered.

"How did you get here then?" Tara asked, curious. "Not that it's out of the norm. You did see our other friends. It's just…" She shrugged. "Curiosity," Tara said as they all climbed into the truck.

"Flew," Selene said easily.

"I can fly too," Tara said a little eagerly.

"You can?" Selene asked.

He drove them back to the hotel while the sisters compared skills. Normally, the entire situation would have been laughable, but he knew it warmed Tara's heart to have someone else like her.

Selene, like Tara, had strength and flight abilities, but had never lit up like Tara had. Instead, she had speed and, according to her, couldn't be cut, shot, or injured in any way. The little trick about light was something she had a difficult time explaining. Apparently, she could fold darkness around her.

"You've never been hurt?" Tara asked as he parked at the hotel.

"Never," Selene said. "I'll go check in."

"We're in room one-eleven. If you want to knock on our door after, we can talk more," Tara said as they climbed out of the truck. Then she walked over and wrapped her arms around Selene again. "I can't tell you how wonderful it is to have you here."

He saw a look of sadness and fear cross Selene's eyes for a brief moment.

"I wish it was under better circumstances," Selene added.

Tara nodded, and then Selene disappeared into the hotel's front office.

"I hate to say it, but it needs to be said. Are you sure we can trust her?" Colt asked once they were in their room.

"There's no doubt in my mind. When she appeared in the field, I just... knew." Tara shrugged. "I didn't know she was coming," she added with a frown. "I felt something building, like I've felt for a while, but when she arrived, it just made sense." Tara sat down on the edge of the bed. "It's like all of the pieces are falling in place. As if it was fate."

"Hey." He knelt before her, taking her hands in his. "We'll get through this. I don't believe everything is written in stone."

Her eyes searched his. "I don't want to lose you."

"You won't," he assured her. "I'm not going anywhere." He pulled her into his arms just as a knock sounded at their door.

CHAPTER 19

Tara sat in the hotel room, looking across the table at her sister. If she hadn't known it in her bones, she would have never imagined that they were related.

Her sister's long hair was dark brown, so dark that it was almost black. Her pale skin was flawless. Her dark eyes seemed to take in everything around her, as if she was untrusting. Sort of like Tara had been when she'd first arrived in town.

The more she looked at Selene, the more she realized they were almost complete opposites.

The moment Selene had appeared in the dark field, she'd felt her. It was as if a part of her that had been missing had fallen into place.

Just like the two moons she'd grown up seeing each night in the sky, she and Selene were each a half of something greater.

"Have you had visits from our parents?" Tara asked Selene.

"Yes," Selene answered with a slight sigh. The southern drawl assured Tara that Selene had spent a great deal of time in the south. "They've been visiting me for years," she added, looking a little weary.

"Any clue what's going to happen tomorrow?" Colt asked.

Selene ran her eyes over him and then shook her head. "No. I've seen visions, but each time they change."

"Same here," Tara admitted.

"In some, Rhea is the destroyer, in others, Typhon is," Selene added. "In others there are different monsters that help them both. The only steady fact in each vision is that nothing survives the battle."

"You mentioned back in the field that you're the goddess of darkness. Why?" Tara asked her.

Selene glanced down at her hands. "It's what Typhon has called me from the beginning. Another gift of mine is that I can't be seen in the dark. No matter how bright the light, it won't penetrate the darkness that surrounds me."

"Where I came from, Selene and Tara were twin moons," Tara said, taking her sister's hand in her own. "They were beacons in the night sky, watching out for and protecting all below."

"Where you come from?" Selene shook her head.

"I'm from another world. I think Mason called it a parallel universe. That's the best way to describe it. Another planet, similar in almost everything to this one." Tara looked at Colt with a smile. "Rhea hid me there, or so she claims. with a man I believed was my father. I had a normal life until my sixteenth birthday, when I appeared here. In this world."

"In your ruined prom dress," Selene added.

"Yes, my party dress," she corrected.

"Must have been some party," Selene said. "I remember being jealous of the dress, even though it was ruined."

Tara wanted to ask her sister why but figured there were more important things to talk about currently.

"Your friends," Selene asked after a moment, "are like us?"

"In a way," Tara answered.

Selene's eyes moved to Colt. "And you?"

"Nope, normal boring human with no extra powers," he answered with a smile.

"That's not necessarily true," Tara said. "We're fated. We've been together all throughout history." She took up his hand.

"Like reincarnation?" Selene asked.

"Something like that," Tara replied. "Whatever it is, we're meant to do this together."

"And the others?" Selene asked.

"Yes, but it's complicated. Some of them have their own families. We don't want to jeopardize that."

Selene was quiet for a moment. "I've seen them before. I spent a lifetime looking..."—she shook her head— "for a sliver of normalcy. For anyone who might understand what I was going through." Her eyes moved up to Tara's, and Tara knew just how she felt. How lonely the last ten years had been.

Reaching over, she wrapped her arms around Selene again.

"You don't have to be alone anymore," she assured Selene. "I'm here." She glanced up and saw Colt standing over them, looking worried. Reaching for him, she pulled him into the hug with Selene. "We're here," she corrected. "You'll meet the rest of the gang tomorrow morning at breakfast." She pulled back. "For now, why don't we get some rest?"

Selene dried her face and nodded. "I'm next door to you."

"If you need us," Colt said softly.

"Thanks." Selene avoided their eyes. "I left in such a hurry when I got your call. I drove straight here."

"My call?" Tara asked, confused.

"A burst of power that showed me exactly where you were. A few days ago."

"Where did you come from, exactly? How far away from Hidden Creek?" Tara asked.

Selene shrugged. "Atlanta. I was… visiting a friend." Selene reached for the door. "Goodnight," she said before disappearing out the door.

Tara turned back to Colt and silently walked into his waiting arms.

"That was… unexpected," Colt said into her hair.

"Yeah," she agreed with a nod of her head. "One last happy surprise." She sighed. "I'm tired."

"Me too. We'd better get some rest," he said, still holding onto her. "Are you okay?"

"Yes," she sighed. "Just… this feels right. Her being here."

"Yeah," he agreed. "She was as lost as you were when we first arrived in town."

His words played over in her head as she lay in his arms, trying to shut down. There was too much to think about. Too much coming their way. Sometime just before dawn, she finally slipped into a dreamless slumber.

She woke when she heard Colt turn off the shower in the bathroom.

Glancing at the clock, she realized she had gotten less than three hours of sleep. Thankfully, she wasn't working that morning and didn't have to be into the coffee shop before sunup.

They were meeting the rest of the gang there at ten, after the main morning rush.

"Morning," Colt said, walking into the room with nothing but a towel draped low on his hips. She felt her body instantly come alive. He was an impressive specimen of a man. Lean toned muscles ran down his stomach. His chest and arms were wide with bulky muscles, as were his thighs. Strong. It was the best word she could think of describe him.

"If you keep looking at me like that, we might be a little

late meeting everyone," Colt said, walking over to sit on the side of the bed.

Smiling, she reached over and pulled him down on top of her.

"Then it looks like we're going to be late," she said before kissing him. She ran her fingers over his still-damp skin, pushing her hands through his wet hair, kissing his warm lips, feeling his hard body next to her softer one.

Here too was contrast, yet they moved in unison with the same goal—pleasing one another and themselves. She'd never felt so connected to anyone in her life.

When he touched her, memories of their past lives together blurred with the now, causing her love to swell beyond her ability to hold it all inside.

When she cried out his name with her release, she knew that together, they held more power than even her parents had assumed. Somehow, with Colt by her side, she just knew that she was going to beat fate. Somehow, she was going to stop the end of the world.

An hour later, she sat in the coffee shop, listening to everyone argue. After they'd introduced Selene to the gang, discussions had started about how they were going to deal with things that night.

Since there was still a handful of other people enjoying their coffees in the shop, their conversations were very vague. At first, it was just everyone asking Selene questions about where she'd come from and her life.

Tara was interested to learn that she'd spent most of her childhood bouncing from foster home to foster home in the Nashville area. She didn't mention the friend she'd been visiting in Georgia, and the rest of the gang didn't ask.

It was as if everyone had been expecting her to appear before tonight. Tara wondered if they had already discussed the possibility.

The moment the group was alone in the shop, Jess locked the door and turned off the open sign.

"I think I can close a few hours early today." She sat down next to Jacob. "We don't mean to pry, but every new member has to go through a little trust test," Jess said, nodding to Xtina.

Xtina sighed heavily, then held out her hands towards Selene. "Do you mind?" Xtina asked.

Selene's dark eyebrows rose slightly. "Things don't go well when people touch my skin," she said.

"Yeah, I forgot to ask you about that last night," Colt said. "Tara didn't seem to be affected."

Selene looked down at her hands. "I guess she's an exception."

"What happens?" Jess asked.

"The best I can tell is that people see their worst nightmares when they touch me," Selene answered. "Sort of a glimpse into their own madness."

"I'll chance it," Xtina said. "Just as long as you don't mind my gift of seeing your memories."

A look of curiosity crossed Selene's face. "Everyone?"

"Everyone except my husband." Xtina smiled and motioned towards Mike.

Selene was quiet for a moment. "There is one person I've never affected besides Tara," she said quietly. The she reached out and laid her hand in Xtina's.

Everyone watched the two women as moments passed by in silence. When Xtina leaned back and broke their connection, everyone relaxed.

"You… didn't see anything?" Selene asked.

"I saw parts of your childhood. The difficulty and loneliness of being passed from one home to another," Xtina said with sadness. "I saw the first time you realized you had a gift. The fear of those around you. How they treated you. I'm so sorry you went through everything you did. I also saw your fear of what's coming and that you would do everything in your power to stop it. Like the rest of us." This last part Xtina said to the table. "We can trust her."

Everyone seemed to relax even further.

"Okay." Jess broke into the silence. "How are we going to do this?"

At eight thirty that evening, Selene, Tara, and Colt stood in the middle of the field where the two women had been conceived. He hadn't been shocked in the slightest when they'd found out earlier that the two sisters were twins.

Even though they looked nothing alike, they had several similarities, mainly in their powers. But where Tara could harness light, Selene gravitated towards darkness. That fact was reflected in their appearances as well. Tara had light blonde hair and tanned skin while Selene had darker hair and pale skin. Even their eyes were opposite. Tara's were soft and green, while Selene had deep hazel eyes.

The question was why had Tara been hidden in a different world, sheltered by a loving family, while Selene had been discarded?

Without Selene's knowledge, Tara and Colt had misled everyone, telling them to meet at the silo. They knew that Joe and Brea would hold to their promises and figured the best course of action was to not even meet everyone down in the silo.

The further the rest of them were from the danger, the better. Besides, Tara didn't think any of them held any real power to fight what was coming.

They had filled Selene in on their plan and, since she was new to the group, explained that it was Tara's game to move what players she had around.

"Put me where you want me," Selene had said with a shrug. "No matter what happens, tonight we'll all be fighting for our lives."

That statement had caused a shiver to race through Colt. And even though he didn't hold any power, there was no way he was going to leave Tara's side. He was prepared to fight to the death, if there was a possibility of saving the world and saving her.

"Are you sure about this?" he asked Tara as they walked through the field.

"No, but it's the best I can do." She looked around. "I won't jeopardize our new friends. Not when I don't have to."

"Why here?" Selene asked when they stopped walking.

"It's where we were conceived," Tara answered, motioning around them.

"My power is stronger at the full moon," Selene replied. "Yours?"

"I… never thought about it. I suppose so." Tara looked down at her hands.

"Long story short, the moon is where the rest of the group locked up Thanatos, the god of death." Colt shrugged.

"Okay." Selene sighed and glanced up to the dark sky. "What time does the moon rise?"

"Eight fifty-one," Tara and Colt replied at the same time.

"What is it we expect to happen, exactly?" Colt asked.

"Darkness will fall," Tara said.

"Is that what you've seen?" Selene asked.

"Yes, you?" Tara asked her.

"Not... exactly," Selene answered slowly. "I've seen several things, all ending in a flash of bright light. Like an explosion."

"That could be—" Tara stopped talking and both sisters tensed and turned to the sky.

"Something's wrong," they said together.

He was standing beside Tara one moment, and in the next, he was lying in the base of the silo, looking up at the group of friends. All ten of them.

"What?" He started to sit up.

"Don't move! Tara and Selene's lives depend on you staying right where you are," Jess said quickly. Before he could blink, another man appeared beside him, a tall blond man in a very expensive business suit.

"What the hell?" the man said, looking around him.

"Somnum," Jess said, motioning to the man. Instantly, the man fell back, his eyes closed.

"He's asleep," Jess assured the others. Then she held her hands high in the air, towards the moon, which was now directly above them. "Veni Rhea. Veni Typhon," Jess said in a loud voice.

In the next second, the light from the full moon was blocked out.

"Keep the circle," Jess said loudly over the rumble of thunder.

One minute, the walls of the silo were surrounding them, then the next, the twelve of them were in the open space of the field with the dark sky above them.

Tara and Selene hovered over the ground, their unconscious bodies floating in the breeze.

"Hecate, why have you summoned us?" a hissing voice echoed loudly in the darkness. "We have come to claim what is ours."

"You cannot have them," Jess said loudly.

"You cannot stop us." This time it was a warm, smooth woman's voice. "There power is needed elsewhere."

"They are needed here," Jess said firmly.

"What do you know of these matters?" Typhon hissed.

He watched Liz step forward, her eyes locked high above them, into the darkness.

"I am oracle," she said loudly. "I have seen what will happen if you remove the sisters from this world."

"We do not concern ourselves with the troubles of one world," Rhea answered.

"Not just this world," Liz answered. "All worlds. Every last one of them." Liz turned to Joleen. "Show them," she said.

Joleen stepped forward. When she reached over and touched Jess's arm, light shot out of Jess's fingers, forming a ball.

A scene unfolded of a world in chaos. Then it flashed to show another scene of more destruction. One after another, thousands of worlds were annihilated as they all watched in horror.

"What brings this destruction?" Rhea asked.

"The lack of balance," Liz answered firmly.

"What you have created was against the will of the gods. As punishment, they will be forever out of your reach. Their power is not yours to have." Jess motioned to Tara and Selene. "They have grown separate, stronger than even you could have foreseen. Yet their powers are connected. If you remove them from existence, their power will be left unchecked."

"We must feed on them," Typhon hissed. "It is our way. If we are to survive, the gods must continue. Their power is ours."

"Each day they grow stronger, and we grow weaker. We cannot do our tasks without what little power we spared to create them long ago," Rhea answered. "We split off, planting the seeds. Now it is our time to harvest."

"I thought you wanted to protect her." Colt screamed. "You had me find her. Why?"

Rhea's eyes turned to his. "You were Tara's last piece to her power. I brought her to this world on her sixteenth birthday in hopes that her power would grow."

"Why hide her in a different world in the first place?" Colt asked.

"Because we are not the only gods looking to feed." Typhon hissed.

"You think that this band of powerful people are safe? You are a growing by the numbers. So much power here is like a beacon in the night." Rhea said with a shake of her head. "More will come for what is here.

"Now, stand aside witch, our daughters are finally strong enough to satisfy our hunger." Typhon bellowed.

"No, you'll have to go through us or find another way to get your power." Jess said sarcastically. "Just don't consume your children."

"We do not consume. Only return them to where they belong. Yes, their powers will be drained temporarily. Which is why they must be reset once more."

"Reset?" Colt asked.

Rhea nodded. "A rebirth of sorts. Each time, they are seeded." She nodded to both Colt and the blonde man asleep by him. "So shall their eternal mates who are their keys to their powers."

All was quiet for a moment.

"Can't you take your powers elsewhere? Aren't you the mother of worlds?" Liz asked.

"I am," Rhea answered. "Which is why I require so much eternal power."

"So if the worlds are destroyed, all of your children will

die," Liz said, laying a hand over her belly. "How can you allow this?"

"Typhon, aren't you the father of monsters? Surely there are a few bad ones with enough power that you can consume instead of these two?" Jess asked, motioning towards Tara and Selene.

"There is another way," Rhea said finally as the winds slowed and the darkness lightened up slightly.

Colt could see the moon breaking through the clouds that had been circling the group.

"Then do that," Liz suggested contemptuously.

"We would need the help of a Hecate," Rhea said.

"I'm willing to help." Jess walked forward.

"No!" Jacob shouted.

Rhea's laughter stopped everyone.

"A special Hecate. You are powerful, yes, but not quite strong enough. We require one that is not quite powerful yet, he must find his mate to give him the strength that is required. It is foretold he will be the strongest Hecate to ever walk the earths," Rhea said.

"Reed," Jess said, her face going pale. "You can't have him…" Jess's eyes filled with tears. "We will fight you."

"Do not worry yourself, Mother Hecate. He will unwillingly help all of the worlds and gods who watch over them when the time comes, the decision will be his alone," Rhea said.

"For now, what can you offer us?" Typhon hissed.

Joleen stepped forward as Jess's tears rolled down her face. "There is a place where Thanatos slumbers. He is powerful and currently is vulnerable."

Loud hissing sounds made Colt and the others cover their ears.

"We despise him," Typhon hissed.

"Good, you know of him," Joleen said with a smile when

the hissing died down.

"Where?" Rhea asked. "This will be an acceptable exchange. His power, even if he is drained temporarily, will suffice us for a time."

"If I send you there," Jess began, wiping the tears from her face, "will you go and leave this place, leave your daughters alone? Never to return?"

"I cannot promise this, Hecate. If we do not take them now, each of our daughters will have to fight other battles," Rhea answered. "Others will seek to gain or control their powers as it continues to grow."

"An immortal god's powers for two mortals?" Jess said. "I'd say that is a pretty good bargain."

"Our daughters are more than just mortals," Typhon hissed. "She is the chosen one." He motioned towards Tara. "And one day Selene will watch over all that is beyond."

"If Thanatos truly slumbers, then you have our promise we will not return until called," Rhea said.

Jess glanced over at Liz, who seemed to be deep in thought. When she blinked and then turned to Jess and nodded, Jess answered.

"Agreed. Release them first. Then I will show you where Thanatos slumbers," Jess said.

Colt watched as both Tara's and Selene's still bodies floated towards the ground.

"My mother, a Hecate, slumbers with Thanatos," Jess said when the sisters lay in the dirt. "Will you release her?"

"Your mother is not our concern. If she has the power to return to you when we drain Thanatos, you can have her," Typhon answered.

Jess looked around the circle of friends and nodded. Instantly, the group started chanting.

Colt glanced up when a bright light caught his attention.

He watched in horror as the full moon grew bigger and bigger until it filled the entire night sky.

"Go," Jess said firmly, pointing to the bright light.

Colt watched as a dark shadow of a man slithered into the light, followed by the form of a woman. They were no more than shadows and when they disappeared, before he could blink, the moon was back to its normal size and high above them.

The moment they were gone, everything flashed and, suddenly, they were back in the silo. Tara's scream echoed in the vast space as she sat up, light shooting from her fingertips, aimed at the sky.

Colt jumped up from the middle of the circle and sprinted over to where she sat on the cement.

"What happened?" Tara asked him, looking around.

"Hell if I know." He held onto her. "But I have you. That's all that matters," he said, vowing to never let her go.

"Tara?" Selene asked, sitting up. "Did we win?"

Jess walked over to them. "We did," she said with a smile. "You might want to go try and explain to your friend why he's in Hidden Creek instead of Atlanta." Jess pointed behind them to the blond man.

"Scott?" Selene said with a frown. "How…" she started to ask. "What happened?"

"I'm tired," Xtina said, getting everyone's attention. "Why don't we head back to our place and fill everyone in on how we bargained to save the world?"

CHAPTER 21

*T*ara sipped the tea and held the hot mug that Xtina had set in front of her. For some reason, she couldn't seem to get her hands warm.

"What do you remember?" Colt asked her.

He was sitting beside her, his arm resting around her shoulders, and she doubted he would leave her side anytime soon. The way he looked at her, his eyes full of worry and love, made her feel warm on the inside.

She looked over at Selene for a brief moment and then made up her mind to tell them only what they needed to hear, knowing her sister would remain quiet.

"The three of us were standing in the field together. Then Selene and I mentioned that something didn't feel right. The next thing I remember you were standing over us," Tara explained.

"That's it?" Colt asked her.

She nodded and glanced around the room. "What happened?"

"I'm afraid it was all my fault," Joleen chimed in.

"Well, it started with me," Liz said. "I did mention I'm an oracle, didn't I?"

"Yes," Tara answered, sinking back into Colt's shoulder.

"That means I can see things. The future, the past, you name it. I knew the moment you decided to cut us out of the fun, what was going to happen. So just before you met with Brea, Ethan, Joe and me, the rest of us had met here." She motioned around the room. "And came up with our plan."

"You made a promise," Tara said with a frown. She remembered sealing the deal.

"Well, the thing about promises…" Jess said, "is that you can't make one if you've already made another that counters the deal. Basically, I got to them first. Besides, everyone knows that you make a pact with a witch before making a pact with a god…" Jess smiled. "The witch trumps a god every time," she finished with a shrug.

Jacob's arm wrapped around Jess's shoulders.

"My wife came up with the plan to call the… your parents. We all knew they were both going to double-cross you," Jacob said.

"It was sort of obvious. You can't trust a god. Ever," Joleen added. "So while Brea brought Colt to the silo, Joe went and got Scott here." She motioned to the blond man who was brooding in the corner of the room. So far, the man hadn't said a word to the group. Selene and he had spoken quietly in the field earlier.

"Who is…" Colt asked.

"Scott Logan," the man said.

"My… a friend," Selene supplied.

"We grew up together," Scott added.

"I knew that the only way to call on the gods was to pull the two of you, Tara and Selene, from them. The spell I used to do that needed the people closest to the two of you," Jess supplied.

"What happened?" Selene asked.

"Your parents came. They overtook you and were prepared to drag you away to consume your… well, you, I guess." Liz shrugged. "No matter what future I saw, I knew that if they took you, everything would end. Whether in darkness, or in light, every world in existence was doomed."

"So, we rescued you," Xtina added.

"How?" Tara asked, feeling a little overwhelmed. The people she'd only known for a little under a month had risked their lives to save her and her sister. To save the world, yet again.

"We made a bargain with them. A sleeping god in exchange for the two of you," Jess answered. A look of worry flashed between her and Jacob. "For now."

"Why us?" Selene asked.

"Yin and yang," Liz answered. "Lightness." She motioned towards Tara. "And darkness." She nodded towards Selene. "The same reason the two of you are more powerful together than apart. You are balance."

"Rhea and Typhon hadn't realized that they'd created the ultimate balance," Joleen said.

"No matter how many lifetimes we've all lived, the one steady factor is that the two of you create stability," Liz said.

Everyone remained silent for a while. Tara finished the tea and felt a little better.

"Do you think it's true what Rhea said? That together, our power is a beacon for others to come?" Xtina asked.

"If so, then I guess we need to start planning for the next time we have to save the world," Jess added.

Each person in the gang nodded. "Agreed," most of them said.

"What about you?" Xtina asked Selene. "Your parents mentioned that the two of you"—she glanced at Tara as well

— "would have more battles. Will you stick around here? Let us help you through whatever is coming?"

Selene glanced over at Scott, who didn't even blink back at her.

"I… have some loose ends to tie up first," Selene said, turning away from the man. "If there's a place for me here…"

"We're moving into a two-bedroom apartment tomorrow," Tara jumped in.

"And opening a restaurant. If you need a job?" Colt offered.

Tara reached over and took his hand, overjoyed that he would so eagerly offer her sister a place in their lives.

"Then I suppose I'll be back after," Selene answered. Suddenly, she turned to Liz. "If you can see ahead that it's the right choice?"

Liz smiled. "It is." Liz's eyes moved to the blond man. "For the both of you."

Tara saw the man tense slightly.

"Thanks," Selene said with a nod. "I think I'll take Scott back to Atlanta."

Selene stood up and walked to the door as Scott followed her.

The blond man stopped at the door. "It was… interesting meeting everyone," Scott said, and then he walked out.

"That man doesn't know it yet, but he'll be back," Liz said with a smile.

"You're scary," Colt joked. "Did you know all of this would happen?" he asked her.

"Yes," Liz said with a smile. "Well, once Tara made up her mind to protect her friends." She laid a hand over her stomach. "All of us."

"You could have told me," Tara suggested.

Liz shook her head. "You would have changed your

tactic." She pointed to her. "I don't know if you know this about yourselves, but you're stubborn."

Tara smiled. "Only some of the time."

"So, I teleported?" Colt asked Brea.

"I teleported," she corrected. "You just came along for the ride. I brought you here from the field."

He chuckled. "I didn't even get some warning. I mean, one minute I was in the field…" He frowned. "How did we all end up in the silo one moment and the field the next? Then back to the silo?"

"That was my doing," Joleen said. "Remember? I can command time and space. Liz mentioned that our powers were stronger in the silo, but in order to be able to push the gods, they had to think they were still in the field, where their powers were strongest."

"So, you projected to everyone that we were in the field?" Colt asked.

"Something like that." Joleen smiled. "Not bad for my first try I'd say."

"On that note," Jess stood up. "I feel the need to hug both of my men. Clara's probably ready for us to pick Reed up."

"We need to pick up Harper as well," Xtina stood.

"I'll get her," Mike offered. "You head up. You've earned the extra sleep." He bent and kissed Xtina.

As everyone shuffled out, she held onto Colt's hand. They caught a ride to where Colt had parked his truck earlier that night, along the road to Xtina's house.

"It's a good thing your friends disobeyed you," he said as he drove into the hotel's parking lot. "You and Selene were apparently no match for your parents."

Tara glanced over at him. "I may have lied a little about what I remember. About what happened after they took you," she admitted.

He turned off the truck and looked at her.

"You did?" His eyes scanned hers.

"Yes. I noticed the moment that you disappeared that I no longer had the power to fight them. Selene and I tried our best. We both fought against the wind, against the storm that had surrounded us. I remembered what you'd found about Typhon, how a bolt of lightning had taken him out."

"Please tell me I didn't miss you throwing a bolt of lightning at a god?" he said, eagerly.

"I tried." She winced. "Which is what apparently knocked both Selene and me out."

"Practice," he assured her. "Maybe you'll get better with practice?"

She smiled. "Don't think you have me fooled." She took his hand in his. "You just think it's hot, a woman who can toss lightning around."

"Hell, yes." He chuckled.

Tara's smile fell away. "I doubt even with you by my side that we would have had enough strength to beat them both. Maybe if it had just been one, but together..." She shook her head. "My parents were too much for just us."

"Apparently, not for your friends. Together, they somehow controlled the two gods. Manipulated and corralled them like they were children," Colt said with a shake of his head. "Not only did they do that, but I'm pretty sure that if they had to, they would have overpowered them. I think Typhon and Rhea knew they were outmatched too." He chuckled. "You should have heard Jess making demands." He sighed. "I think they're afraid of witches."

"Together, I have a feeling the group can do anything. It's one of the reasons I think I'm going to like staying in Hidden Creek," she admitted. "I know you're committed to opening your restaurant..."

"I'm committed to you," he said, taking her hand in his. "If you're staying, then so am I." He pulled her into a kiss.

Two months later...

Tara held Colt's hand for one moment more.

"Ready?" she asked him, admiring the crisp white chef's attire he wore.

"As much as I can be," he admitted, pulling on his shirt.

She dropped his hand and watched as he walked over to unlock the front doors of the Harvest Moon Family Restaurant.

In the past two months, with their friends' help, they had transformed the business into a family friendly dining experience. It had taken a lot of debating amongst the friends on what to call the place. In the end, they picked a name that best suited the group. Since they were the reason she and Colt were sticking around town, they figured it was only fair for the group to have a say in the name.

She and Colt had moved into their apartment upstairs and had enjoyed shopping for furniture to fill the space.

Now, the line of people who had formed outside the doors shuffled in. Tara greeted each group and helped seat everyone at the tables she and Colt had purchased at a secondhand store just outside of Atlanta.

They hadn't seen Selene in town again since that night. She's had a call from her a few days after. Selene was trying to close out her life in Tennessee so she could move down there and start her new life in Hidden Creek.

"I think we're going to need to hire more help," she told Colt, half an hour after they had opened their doors.

"On it. I had two more people apply." Colt smiled at her. "One of them was a sous chef."

She gave him the new order and kissed him quickly before heading back out to deliver a table's meals.

The whole gang had been there when they'd opened the doors.

Jess, Jacob, Reed, and Clara sat at a table right up front. While she was dropping off their food, the door opened behind her, and she glanced over to see Selene walk inside, a worried look in her dark eyes.

Smiling, Tara walked over and hugged her sister. "You're back," she said with some relief.

"I am, but not for long," Selene said, worry filling her voice. "I came back to get some help. Scott's been taken."

"Taken?" Tara gasped. "By whom?"

Selene frowned and answered. "Our brother."

Breaking Travis

Roping Ryan

Wild Bride

Corey's Catch

Tessa's Turn

Saving Trace

Christmas Holly

The Grayton Series

Last Resort

Someday Beach

Rip Current

In Too Deep

Swept Away

High Tide

Sunset Dreams

Lucky Series

Unlucky In Love

Sweet Resolve

Best of Luck

A Little Luck

Christmas Wish

Silver Cove Series

Silver Lining

French Kiss

Happy Accident

Hidden Charm

A Silver Cove Christmas

Sweet Surrender

Second Chances

Entangled Series – Paranormal Romance

The Awakening

The Beckoning

The Ascension

The Presence

The Calling

The Chosen

Haven, Montana Series

Closer to You

Never Let Go

Holding On

Coming Home

The Hard Way

Pride Oregon Series

A Dash of Love

My Kind of Love

Season of Love

Tis the Season

Dare to Love

Where I Belong

Because of Love

A Thing Called Love

First Comes Love

Someone to Love

Wildflowers Series

Summer Nights

Summer Heat

Summer Secrets

Summer Fling

Summer's End

Summer's Wish

Distracted Series

Wake Me

Tame Me

Stand Alone Books

Twisted Rock

Hope Harbor

Raven Falls

For a complete list of books:

http://JillSanders.com

ABOUT THE AUTHOR

Jill Sanders is a New York Times, USA Today, and international best-selling author of Sweet Contemporary Romance, Romantic Suspense, Western Romance, and Paranormal Romance novels. With over 75 books in eleven series, translations into several different languages, and audiobooks there's plenty to choose from. Look for Jill's bestselling stories wherever romance books are sold or visit her at jillsanders.com

Jill comes from a large family with six siblings, including an identical twin. She was raised in the Pacific Northwest and later relocated to Colorado for college and a successful IT career before discovering her talent for writing sweet and sexy page-turners. After Colorado, she decided to move south, living in Texas and now making her home along the Emerald Coast of Florida. You will find that the settings of several of her series are inspired by her time spent living in these areas. She has two sons and off-set the testosterone in her house by adopting three furry little ladies that provide her company while she's locked in her writing cave. She enjoys heading to the beach, hiking, swimming, wine-tasting, and pickleball with her husband, and of course writing. If you have read any of her books, you may also notice that there is a love of food, espe-

cially sweets! She has been blamed for a few added pounds by her assistant, editor, and fans... donuts or pie anyone?

facebook.com/JillSandersBooks
twitter.com/JillMSanders
amazon.com/Jill-Sanders/e/B009M2NFD6?tag=jillmcom-20
bookbub.com/authors/jill-sanders